Whatever After

SEEING RED

Read all the Whatever After books!

Whatever After

SEEING RED

SARAH MLYNOWSKI

Scholastic Inc.

Copyright © 2018 by Sarah Mlynowski

This book was originally published in hardcover by Scholastic Press in 2018.

All rights reserved. Published by Scholastic Inc., *Publishers since 1920.* SCHOLASTIC and associated logos are trademarks and/or registered trademarks of Scholastic Inc.

The publisher does not have any control over and does not assume any responsibility for author or third-party websites or their content.

This book is a work of fiction. Names, characters, places, and incidents are either the product of the author's imagination or are used fictitiously, and any resemblance to actual persons, living or dead, business establishments, events, or locales is entirely coincidental.

ISBN 978-1-338-16294-3

10 9 8 7 6 5 4 3 2 1   20 21 22 23 24

Printed in the U.S.A.   40

This edition first printing 2020

for chloe. i don't know where your path will take you, but i know it will be somewhere amazing.

chapter one

Nana's Here!

Yes! It's Friday at three P.M.

I know exactly what you're thinking. That I'm happy because it's the weekend. No school for two days. No quizzes. No cold cafeteria chicken nuggets. No waiting for the swing hogs to give me and my friends our turn at recess.

And that's all true. But the *real* reason I'm so excited right now?

Guess who's waiting outside to pick up me and my brother from school?

NANA!

Yep. Nana!

My grandmother is amazing. She's nice and fun and so smart. She's a professor at a college in Chicago. That's where I *used* to live, before my family moved here, to Smithville. So we don't get to see Nana too often. In fact, we haven't seen her since we moved.

"There she is!" I exclaim, pointing at Nana's yellow Jeep, parked in front of our school. Nana gets out of her incredibly cool rental car with a huge grin on her face. She's short, with curly gray hair that comes to her chin, and bright hazel eyes.

"Nana!" Jonah shouts with glee, and goes rushing over.

"There's my big boy!" Nana says, picking him up and swinging him around.

Jonah's only seven, and hasn't reached the age where he'd get embarrassed by that kind of thing.

"And my Abby!" Nana exclaims, grabbing me in a bear hug.

I might be ten, but hey, Nana gives the best hugs.

"I'm so happy you're here," I tell her.

Nana's staying with us this whole weekend while my parents are away at a work conference.

"Are you all set to go home?" Nana asks, opening the back door of the Jeep.

I nod happily. I already said good-bye to my two best friends, Frankie and Robin, before dashing outside the school.

"I bet we're having breakfast for dinner, right?" Jonah says excitedly as he hops into the car.

Nana laughs. "Of course we are. French toast with butter and maple syrup, and fresh-picked strawberries from my garden that I brought all the way from Chicago."

"I love breakfast for dinner," I say. This is already the best day ever.

As I get in next to Jonah, I glance at Nana's tote bag on the front seat. Sticking halfway out of the bag is a thick hardcover book with a dark blue cover and gold trim. Ooh! I'd know that book anywhere. It's *The Big Book of Fairy Tales*. The book must have a hundred stories in it. Nana has been reading fairy tales to me and Jonah since we were toddlers. Maybe even babies.

"I see you brought our favorite book," I say as I buckle in.

"Sure did," Nana says, getting into the driver's seat. "I'll read you guys a story or two before bed. If you're still interested in fairy tales, that is."

"Of course we're still interested!" Jonah says, raising his eyebrows at me. "VERY interested. Right, Abby?"

I put my finger to my lips. "Shhh!" I whisper.

Nana glances at us in the rearview mirror, looking a little confused.

Okay, yes. Jonah and I are both acting a little weird.

Why? Because we actually go INTO fairy tales.

More like FALL into them.

Seriously.

Cinderella. Snow White. Aladdin. The Princess and the Pea. Those are just a few of the fairy tales we've visited.

See, we have a magic mirror in our basement. When we knock on it three times at midnight, it pulls us inside and whisks us into a fairy tale.

Usually. The mirror doesn't always let us in.

But if it starts to hiss, and then turns purple and swirls, off to fairy tale land we go. Me and Jonah and our cute little brown-and-white dog, Prince.

Nana has no idea. No grown-ups know about the magic

4

mirror. But it's thanks to Nana that I'm so familiar with the fairy tales we end up in. And knowing all the fairy tales can really come in handy, especially when Jonah and I are trying to figure out what's supposed to happen next in a story.

"So tell me *everything* about your lives in Smithville," Nana says to me and Jonah as she drives us home.

And we do. We tell her about our school and our friends and Prince. But of course, we don't mention the magic mirror in our basement. (Or the fact that we got Prince from a fairy tale.)

At home, Nana, Jonah, and I play two rounds of badminton in the backyard, and I'm having so much fun that I don't even mind that Jonah beats me. Twice. (Okay, maybe I mind a little, but I don't want to be a sore loser in front of Nana.) Then we take Prince on a walk. Nana and Prince obviously love each other. Nana keeps rubbing his furry, floppy ears, and Prince wags his tail every time.

When we get back to our house, the phone is ringing in the kitchen. I run to answer it while Jonah settles Prince on his dog bed in the corner of the kitchen. Meanwhile, Nana is taking out the eggs and bread to make her amazing French toast.

I grab the phone. "Hello?"

"Abby? It's Penny."

That's a surprise. Penny is friends with *my* best friend Robin. But Penny and I aren't exactly close friends ourselves. Even if she did go into a story with me once.

"Hi, Penny," I say uncertainly. "What's up?"

"Sooo," Penny says, and I can picture her sitting in her huge bedroom, playing with her blond ponytail. "Since I got an eighty-nine — which is almost an A — on the vocabulary quiz, I'm allowed to have three friends over for a sleepover tonight. I already invited Robin, of course — she IS my best friend — and she said you're good at making s'mores, so you can come, too, if you want. Oh, and I'm inviting Frankie since she tells good ghost stories."

I roll my eyes at only being invited for my s'mores skills. But YAY! A sleepover! S'mores and ghost stories and my two best friends. How fun is that going to be?

"That sounds great," I say. "I just need to check with my nana. She's watching me and Jonah this weekend. But I'm sure she'll say yes."

"Call me back as soon as you can," Penny says impatiently. "We'll be making gourmet pizzas and sundaes. Oh, and ice cream crepes for breakfast. Pickup is at noon tomorrow. Bye!" *Click.*

I rush over to Nana with the phone still in my hand and tell her all about Penny's invitation.

"Doesn't that sound awesome?" I ask Nana.

"It does sound nice," Nana agrees, taking out the whisk and beating the eggs in a silver mixing bowl. "Your friend will be disappointed to hear you can't attend."

Wait. WHAT?

I tilt my head. "What do you mean? Why can't I go?"

"Family time!" Nana says brightly. "You, me, and Jonah."

A bark comes from the direction of Prince's dog bed.

"And Prince," Jonah adds.

"Of course, Prince!" Nana says with a smile.

My cheeks heat up. I do want to spend time with my nana. But she is here until Sunday night. And we've already spent some quality time together! We played two rounds of badminton!

"Nana, I really want to go," I say. "There will be pizzas and sundaes. Plus s'mores and ghost stories. And ice cream crepes in the morning."

"That reminds me," Nana says. "I stopped at Bagel Heaven before I picked you guys up from school." She points to the brown bag on the counter. "We're having bagels tomorrow morning! Poppy seed for you, sesame for Jonah, and an everything bagel for me. Plus a plain one for Prince."

Why is Nana talking about bagels at a moment like this? This is a crisis!

"Nana, please tell me I can go to Penny's?" I beg.

Please say yes. Pleeeeeeeeze!

"I'm sorry, Abby, but no," Nana tells me, dipping a slice of bread into the egg mixture she's whipped up.

"You don't even like Penny," Jonah reminds me.

I frown at Jonah. "I like her sometimes!" I say to him. Then I look back at my nana. Maybe I can talk her into it. I just have to lay out the facts. My parents are lawyers, and that's how they win their trials. By pleading their cases. When I grow up, I want to be a lawyer, too — well, I want to be a judge, but you have to be a lawyer first — so this will be good practice.

"It's a sleepover," I explain to Nana, "and my two best friends will be there. I don't want to be left out."

Nana shakes her head. "I came to spend time with you, Abby. So the answer is no. Maybe you can sleep over next weekend."

Penny isn't having a sleepover NEXT weekend. She's having a sleepover THIS weekend. She's having a sleepover TONIGHT.

"But I'm going to miss all the stuff," I say. "They're going to stay up late telling secrets and I won't know anything!"

"We can stay up late telling secrets," Nana says.

Nanas are for hugs and bedtime stories. Not for secrets.

"I'll get out the strawberries," Jonah offers.

"Thank you, sweetheart," Nana says to him.

"So I really can't go?" I ask Nana with my best puppy-dog eyes. That means they get very round and wide and match the hopeful smile on my face.

"No," she says. There's a slight DO NOT ASK ME AGAIN edge to her tone.

Crumbs.

I call Penny. The numbers take forever to press. I sigh three times. When Penny answers, I explain I can't go.

"Oh, you poor thing," Penny says. "Missing all the fun. We're going to have a disco party at midnight! And we'll be making friendship anklets with these amazing beads my dad picked up in France. You'll be the only one without one. Oh, well. Bye!" *Click.*

Arrrrgh! Boo! Hissss!

She's the worst.

I want to make an anklet, and I want s'mores and ghost stories. I want to hang out with Frankie and Robin at a sleepover — even if Penny has to be there, too.

"Abby, be a sweetie and get out the orange juice, will you?" Nana asks.

I grumble to myself as I head to the refrigerator. I am not feeling very sweet. I am actually feeling extremely bitter.

So maybe Nana's French toast was ooey-gooey delicious. But I'm still really, *really* mad about missing the sleepover.

There is no way I can handle Robin and Frankie having matching friendship anklets with Penny and not me. No. Way.

After we eat popcorn and watch the latest Wonder Woman movie, Nana clicks off the TV. "Wow, how did it get to be so late?" Nana exclaims. "It's definitely past Jonah's bedtime, and it's almost Abby's."

"I love getting to stay up late when you babysit," Jonah says, holding up his hand for a high five.

Nana slaps him five. "That's what nanas are for. A little rule-breaking is always in order."

"If rule-breaking is in order, maybe I can go to the sleepover after all?" I suggest, holding my breath.

"Abby," Nana says, giving me a bit of a frown. "The answer is no, and that's final. No more asking. It's late, anyway. The girls are probably asleep."

They are definitely not asleep.

"Come on, guys," Nana says. "Let's head upstairs. I'll read you both a fairy tale."

Even though I love fairy tales, right now I don't feel like hearing one. That's how I know I'm really upset.

While Nana gets *The Big Book of Fairy Tales*, Jonah and I go into our rooms to change into pj's, and then we meet in Jonah's room. Nana reads us a story I've never heard, about a princess who doesn't have any friends. Probably because she was never allowed to go to sleepovers.

Finally, it's lights-out. Nana tucks in Jonah, kisses him on the forehead, and then comes into my room to tuck me in.

"You do understand, right, Abby?" Nana says, sitting on the edge of my bed. "Family time is important. There will be lots of sleepovers, but we don't get to see each other very often."

"I know," I say, my throat tightening. "I just . . . even if I went to the sleepover, we would have all day tomorrow and Sunday together. That's way more than enough family time."

Nana lifts her chin. "Well," she says in an *I'm very disappointed in you* voice, "it's not enough *for me*. I haven't seen you in months, and I want to spend time with you. You're my favorite granddaughter. My only granddaughter." She leans over to kiss me on the forehead, then stands up. "Okay? Good night, Abby."

"I wish Mom and Dad were here," I say, tears burning the backs of my eyelids. "They would have let me go."

I turn over onto my stomach and bury my face in my pillow so I don't cry.

"You're being rude right now, Abby," Nana says in a quiet voice. "That's not the Abby I know. I hope you'll apologize in the morning."

She walks out of the room, leaving the door slightly ajar.

I'm suffocating myself in the pillow, so I throw it on the floor and flip over onto my back. I sigh and stare up at the ceiling. I'll never fall asleep. I'll be too busy thinking about the midnight disco party and the fancy French anklets.

If only I could sneak over to Penny's house without Nana even knowing.

I sit upright.

Wait a minute.

Would the magic mirror take me? If I asked Maryrose really nicely? Like really, really nicely?

Maryrose is the fairy who's trapped inside our mirror. She's the one who takes me and Jonah into different fairy tales.

How awesome would it be if Maryrose sent me to Penny's? I could just pop right into the middle of their disco party!

I'd be like, *Hey, guys! I've been here the whole time!*

And then I could sneak back to my house in the morning.

I look at my clock. In two hours, it will be midnight.

Magic mirror, here I come.

chapter two

Away We Go

My eyes pop open at 11:54 P.M. Good. I had set my alarm for 11:55, but now I won't have to worry about Nana hearing it go off. If she did, she might come to my room to investigate, and that would ruin my whole plan.

I turn off the alarm, throw back my covers, and scramble out of bed. I glance down at myself. I'm in my pajamas with the little bulldogs on them that Nana sent me for Hanukkah. I might be mad at Nana, but I love these pj's. And it makes sense for me to be in pj's for the sleepover party anyway, right?

I stuff my feet into sneakers and rush out of my room into the hallway.

"What are you doing?" asks a sleepy voice.

I jump.

It's Jonah, standing in the doorway of his room. What is HE doing awake at almost midnight?

"I heard you moving around," he tells me, rubbing his eyes. He has total bedhead — his curly brown hair is all messed up. He's wearing his soccer-ball pajamas that Nana sent *him* for Hanukkah.

"I'm going to Penny's sleepover," I tell Jonah, smoothing down my own messy brown curls. Then I turn to head downstairs.

"What? No!" Jonah gasps, grabbing my arm. "Are you going to walk over in your pajamas in the middle of the night? You can't do that!"

I shake my arm loose. "No, silly. I'm going to take the mirror!"

Jonah snort-laughs. "The mirror? Maryrose isn't going to send you to Penny's. She doesn't take requests. And Penny doesn't live in a fairy tale. Her house is big, but it's not a *real* castle."

16

I flush. "Maryrose *might* send me there. If I ask nicely. Really, really nicely."

"What if Nana checks on you and you're gone?" Jonah demands.

"Why would she check on me? She doesn't know about the mirror." I gesture to my parents' room down the hall, where Nana is staying. "And she's fast asleep! She's tired! She's old!"

"I'm coming downstairs with you," he says.

"Jonah —" I start.

Before I can tell him I'm going alone, he runs into his room and comes back with his sneakers and a hoodie on. Then he rushes past me down the stairs.

"You are *not* coming to Penny's with me!" I whisper-yell. Showing up at the sleepover with my little brother is not what I have in mind. No one wants a little brother at a sleepover. Especially someone else's little brother.

"If Maryrose says she's sending you to Penny's, I won't come!" Jonah whisper-yells back over his shoulder.

Ruff! Prince barks, bounding out of Jonah's room and following my brother downstairs.

This is getting out of hand.

"Shhh!" I say, heading after Jonah and Prince. "You guys better not wake up Nana!"

The three of us hurry down the first flight of stairs, around the corner, and down the basement steps.

"Stay back," I tell Jonah and Prince as I come to a stop right in front of the mirror.

The mirror is huge — bigger than me and bolted onto the wall. The frame is made of stone and decorated with fairies and wands. The mirror came with the house when we moved in. Can you believe the people who lived here before us just left it there? Major score for us.

I glance at my watch. It's exactly midnight. Perfect! I love being punctual.

I knock on the glass three times.

"Hi, Maryrose," I say to the mirror. "It's Abby! Can you take me to Penny's house? Please? Pretty please? Pretty please with maple syrup and strawberries on top?"

The mirror starts to hiss. Then a purple light radiates from the glass. Finally, the glass starts to swirl.

"It's working!" I say, feeling a rush of excitement. "She's going to take me! She's going to take me!" I glance over my shoulder at Jonah. "Do not come with me. Do you hear me? Do not come with me!"

"You don't know that the mirror is taking you to Penny's," Jonah argues. "Abby, listen. You're mad at Nana and not thinking clearly —"

Prince barks his agreement.

They don't know what they're talking about. Maryrose is taking me to Penny's. I just know it.

"Do not come!" I tell my brother again. And then I jump in.

Thump!

Ouch. I land on my hands and knees, and feel the scrape of rough wood against my palms. Wood?

Please be Penny's basement. Please be Penny's basement.

I dust off my pj's and stand up and then —

AHHHHHHH!

I'm staring right into the open eyes of a deer. Seriously.

I jump back. Wait. It's the entire head of a deer.

A head of a deer?

I take a closer look at the animal. Oh. It's actually a *stuffed* deer head mounted on the wall. Not that that's any less scary. But at least it won't eat me.

I cringe and glance away from its glassy amber eyes. BIG MISTAKE! Because now I'm staring at a stuffed brown bear head, also hung on the wall.

And the bear does not look happy.

The room is full of dead animals! Hung like trophies! Gross, gross, gross!

Where am I? *Could* this be a room in Penny's house? A room I've never been inside? A room she has never shown me because she knows I'd be creeped out by all the dead animal heads?

"Excuse me!" I hear a man's voice say loudly behind me. "What are you doing here —"

I freeze. Then I hear a sudden loud THUMP, followed by a familiar voice.

"Abby?"

I spin around and see Jonah sitting at a weird angle on the ground. His eyes are wide, and Prince is clutched in his arms.

"Oh! Why are you here?" I ask my brother. "I told you not to come!"

Then I notice why Jonah is sitting at a weird angle. He's on top of a man. A passed-out man. A passed-out man with bright red hair and a scruffy beard, who's wearing a green vest. That must be the man who spoke to me before!

"Jonah!" I cry, pointing down at the man. "What . . . who . . . is he okay?"

Jonah's eyes are getting even wider. "I don't know! When I went through the portal, I landed on him, and I think he hit his head."

I run over to peer down at the man. His eyes are closed. "Is he . . ." I'm afraid to ask. Prince whimpers worriedly.

"He's breathing," Jonah says, leaning close to the man's face. "I think I just knocked him unconscious."

Sure enough, the man lets out a long *"Snooooooort"* sound, like he's fast asleep.

"You pulled a *Wizard of Oz*!" I tell Jonah.

"Huh?"

"Remember when Dorothy's house lands on top of the witch?"

"No," Jonah says.

"Well, that's what you did. Except he's not a witch."

"And I'm not a house," Jonah points out.

"I wonder who he is," I say, looking at the unconscious man again. "Do you think he's Penny's dad?"

Jonah glances around. "No way. We're definitely not in Penny's house."

"How do you know for sure?" I ask him.

"Um, the dead animal heads?"

"Penny might have dead animal heads," I say.

Prince flattens his ears and growls at the animal heads. I know how he feels.

Jonah points to a window. "It's the middle of the day. We didn't *time*-travel to Penny's."

True. It *is* bright outside.

"We must be in a fairy tale!" Jonah says. "See? Aren't you glad I came now?"

"I am," I have to admit. "Thank you for not listening to me before. So, if we're in a fairy tale . . . which one are we in?"

I look around the room more slowly now. It's a strange room, even aside from the animal heads. Everything in it — the bed, the desk, the chair — looks to be made out of tree bark. I can even see that there's a tree-bark kitchen and a tiny tree-bark bathroom down the hall. Plus, there's a giant tree trunk growing straight out of the floor.

"What is this place?" I wonder out loud. "Is it a beanstalk?"

"A beanstalk?" Jonah asks excitedly, scrambling up off the passed-out man. "Are we finally in *Jack and the Beanstalk*?" My brother cheers. Then his face falls. "Don't tell me I landed on Jack! Ahhh! Did I break Jack?"

"Never mind. It doesn't look like a beanstalk," I say quickly. "I'm sure that's not Jack. And you didn't break him."

Jonah's shoulders relax. "Phew. I mean, I feel bad for this guy, whoever he is. But I would be super sad to have broken Jack."

I notice a bunch of bows and arrows stacked against the wall.

"Could we be in *Robin Hood*?" I ask.

"I love *Robin Hood*!" Jonah cheers again. Then his face falls again. "Don't tell me I broke Robin Hood! That's almost as bad as breaking Jack!"

I study the stuffed animal heads. "Actually, I don't think Robin Hood is a hunter . . ."

The passed-out guy gives another loud *"Snoooooooort"* sound.

"We should really call a doctor," I say. Thankfully, just then, I spot a phone on the wooden desk. Whew. I run over and pick up the receiver. There is only one symbol on it, a star, so I press it.

The line rings twice, and then a woman answers.

"Howlton Help Line, this is Mona," she says cheerfully. "How are you, Huntsman?"

"Huntsman?" I repeat.

"Yes! I have caller ID," Mona says.

"Oh! So I'm not in Robin Hood's house?"

"Who's Robin Hood?"

"Or Jack's house?" I ask, just to make sure.

"I don't know a Jack, either," Mona replies. "But you're calling from the huntsman's house, am I right?"

"You are," I say. "I'm Abby. And I . . . came to visit the . . . um . . . huntsman. But I think he hit his head and is unconscious. Can you send a doctor?"

"Oh! Sure. No problem. Help is on the way!"

Mona hangs up.

I look at Jonah. He looks at me. Prince barks.

"What story has a huntsman?" I ask. "I mean, *Snow White* does, but we've already been there — and it didn't look anything like this."

I notice a small wooden doorway straight ahead. I walk over, open it carefully, and look down. Way down. Wow. We're up high in the air. Like twenty or thirty feet off the ground. We're in a forest full of huge trees with enormous branches and dark green leaves. The sky is bright blue, not a cloud in sight. And the temperature feels just right, like the most perfect spring day.

Jonah comes to join me by the doorway and peers outside. "Abby, we're in a tree house!" he exclaims.

He's right. But this isn't like any tree house I've ever been in. My best friend Frankie has a tree house, but *hers* doesn't have a whole tree trunk shooting up inside of it. And of course, hers doesn't have dead animal decorations — or an unconscious huntsman.

"Hey, there's another tree house," Jonah says, pointing across the way. This tree house has a WEL C OME sign on the outside wall, along with a bird feeder. Two little bluebirds are nibbling at birdseed. The window frames are painted a lemon yellow.

I'd bet that tree house has normal things inside. Like vases. And paintings. And conscious people.

"Snoooooooooooort," says the huntsman, still asleep.

"And there's another," Jonah says, pointing to the left. This tree house has a clothesline going from it to another tree. I can see pairs of pants and a bunch of socks moving in the gentle breeze.

All the tree houses — including the one we're in — have long wooden ladders that go straight down from their door-ways through the leaves and branches.

Okay, we're in a forest full of tree houses. Which fairy tale has tree houses?

Suddenly, I hear a sound coming from the forest below.

"La la la la!" a girl's voice trills.

"I hear singing," I say.

Prince barks, running over to us and looking down.

"Me too," Jonah says, straining to listen.

"La, la, la, a tasty treat. La, la, la, she'll get something to eat," the girl sings.

The singing gets louder.

I squint down through the branches. Now I can see the girl, the one who's singing. She's wearing a long red hoodie and walking on a path through the forest. She's swinging something in her hands . . . a basket? Yep, a wicker picnic basket.

Oh, wait, she's not wearing a hoodie. It's more like a cape with a hood —

"A hood!" I holler. "A red hood!"

"So we are in *Robin Hood*!" Jonah exclaims. "Is that him? He has such a high voice, huh?"

Jonah is going to be disappointed. Because that is NOT Robin Hood.

Only one person wears a red hood in a fairy tale.

chapter three

What's in a Name?

t hat's Little Red Riding Hood!" I tell Jonah triumphantly.

Jonah glances back down into the forest. By now, Little Red Riding Hood has almost disappeared from view.

"But . . . but . . . but . . ." Jonah makes a sad face. "Wasn't she wearing a cape? Maybe it was Supergirl?" he asks hopefully.

I shake my head. "Come on. Girl in a red hood? Forest path? A hunter?" I pause. "Isn't any of this ringing a bell?"

"Nope," Jonah says.

I sigh. He never paid much attention when Nana read us stories from her book of fairy tales. Good thing *I* was listening.

"We're in the story of *Little Red Riding Hood*," I tell him. I've always liked this story.

A girl. A basket of food. A wolf. A nana.

A nana.

I shift from foot to foot, suddenly feeling a teensy bit guilty for sneaking out on *my* nana.

But she was being a little unreasonable. A lot unreasonable.

So I don't feel *that* guilty.

"Let's go say hi to Super-Red!" Jonah says, picking up Prince.

I laugh. "That's not her name."

"Little Red Riding Hood can't be her real name, either," Jonah argues. "No one is named Little Red Riding Hood." He puts one foot on the ladder to head down.

"Wait," I say, pulling Jonah back. "We can't just go up to her! And we can't leave the unconscious huntsman!"

"But a doctor is coming."

True. "But remember, Jonah, we don't know why we're here or what we're supposed to do."

"Do we ever?" he asks.

Also true.

"We always get sent into a story for a reason," Jonah points out. "Maybe we're supposed to help Super-Red." He pauses. "Wait. Is hers the story where the wolf huffs and puffs and blows her house down?"

I giggle. "No. That's *The Three Little Pigs*."

He scratches his head. "Oh. There IS a wolf in *Little Red Riding Hood*, though, right?"

I nod.

"Is the wolf nice or mean?" Jonah asks.

"Have you ever heard of a nice wolf?"

"I guess not," Jonah says.

"This one is a sneaky wolf," I say.

A sneaky, hungry wolf that might be out there in the forest. I shiver.

I glance at the huntsman's walls again. The one animal head I wouldn't mind seeing up there . . . isn't. Which means the wolf is probably somewhere outside. Waiting. Oh, and did I mention hungry?

"Can you tell me the story?" Jonah asks. "Better if I know what's going on."

I close my eyes for a second to remember it. And the weirdest thing happens. It's like I can almost hear my nana reading the story to us. It was just last year when we still lived near Nana, and saw her all the time.

"Okay," I say, sitting down on the edge of the bed. "Here's how the story goes."

Jonah turns the desk chair to face me and sits down with Prince in his lap.

"Little Red Riding Hood's grandmother is sick," I begin, "so —"

"I bet it's Renee," Jonah says.

I frown. "What's Renee?"

"Little Red Riding Hood's name."

"Why?"

"Because it starts with an R. It seems like she should have an R name, right?"

"I don't know, Jonah!" I say.

"Or maybe her name really is just Red. Is anyone named Red?"

"No one I've ever met."

"Do you know what would be really confusing?" Jonah asks.

I sigh. "What?"

"If her name was *another* color. Like Yellow. Or Orange."

"Do you know a lot of people named Yellow or Orange?" I ask.

He shakes his head. "I don't."

"There aren't a lot of kids named after colors," I say.

"No." Jonah pauses. "Oh! Oh! Violet!"

"Good one," I admit. "Should I go on?"

He gives me a thumbs-up.

"ANYWAY," I say. "Little Red Riding Hood's grandma is sick. Little Red Riding Hood's mom gives her a basket filled with food. Her mom tells her to deliver the basket to her grandma, who lives in a cabin in the woods."

"Do you think she calls her grandma Nana, too?" Jonah asks.

"I don't know. We will add that to our list of questions."

"Maybe she calls her something fun like Mee-maw."

I pause. "Mee-maw?"

"Isaac calls his nana Mee-maw!" Jonah raises his hand. "I have another question for our list."

"Yes?"

"What kind of food does Little Red Riding Hood's mom pack in the basket?" Jonah asks.

I don't remember. "Cake, maybe? With tea?"

Jonah licks his lips. "I wish I had cake right now. Chocolate cake with chocolate icing. Or confetti cake with lots of sprinkles inside. Do you think that's what she packed?"

"Jonah, maybe we can find out faster if I finish the story?"

He takes his finger and pulls it across his lips to pretend-zip his mouth.

"Sooo," I go on, "Little Red Riding Hood's mother warns her to stay on the path through the woods. Because there's a wolf out there. And the wolf may sniff out the food."

"Wolves like cake?" Jonah asks.

I shrug. "Who doesn't like cake?"

"Good point," he says.

"So Little Renee —"

Jonah laughs.

I wink and continue. "— stays on the path to her grandma's house. But she has no idea that the wolf is watching her every move. He wants the food she has. And he also wants to gobble up Little Red Riding Hood. But he realizes she might be going someplace where there will be *more* people who he can eat for lunch. So —"

"Wow," Jonah says. "The wolf is greedy, huh? If I ate that many people for lunch, I'd totally throw up."

"Um, you'd probably throw up if you ate any people."

Jonah nods. "True."

"The wolf stops to say hi to Little Red Riding Hood," I continue, "and he asks her where she's going. She tells him she's on her way to her sick grandma's to deliver a snack. The wolf makes a plan. He wants to stall Little Red Riding Hood."

"Why?" Jonah asks.

"Getting to that. See, the wolf tells Little Red Riding Hood she should bring some wildflowers to her grandma since she's sick. Little Red Riding Hood thinks that's a nice idea. But it would mean getting off the path to pick the flowers."

"Her mom told her NOT to get off the path, though," Jonah says.

"Exactly. But she really wants to bring her grandma some pretty flowers. So she goes off the path to collect them."

Jonah leans forward. "And then?"

"While Little Red Riding Hood is picking flowers, the wolf rushes over to Grandma's cabin in the woods. He knocks on the door. And when Grandma asks who it is, he says it's Little Red Riding Hood. So Grandma tells him to come right in."

"Uh-oh," Jonah says.

"Uh-oh is right!" I agree. "The wolf sees Grandma lying in her bed and gobbles her up. Then, knowing that Little Red Riding Hood will arrive any minute, he puts on Grandma's bathrobe and her sleeping cap —"

Jonah opens his mouth, but before he can ask his question, I add, "No, I don't know what a sleeping cap is *exactly*, but I imagine it looks like a shower cap."

He closes his mouth.

"Anyway, the wolf is pretending to be Grandma. So when Little Red Riding Hood gets to her grandmother's house, she goes inside and sees her grandma in bed. But when Little Red comes closer, she thinks her grandma looks sort of different."

"Sort of?" Jonah cries.

I laugh. "Maybe Little Renee needs glasses. But the wolf tells her to come closer. And Little Red Riding Hood says, 'My, Grandma, what a deep voice you have!' And the wolf says, 'The better to greet you with, my dear.'"

"Doesn't Little Red Riding Hood know what her grandma's voice sounds like?" Jonah asks.

"You'd think," I say. "But her grandma IS sick, so maybe she just thinks her voice is hoarse. My voice gets hoarse when I'm sick."

"You sound like a frog when you're sick."

"So do you!" I point out.

"Then what happens?" Jonah asks.

"Little Red Riding Hood comes closer to the bed and sees tall, pointy, furry ears sticking up out of the cap. She says, 'My, Grandma, what big ears you have.'"

"Nana would NOT like if we said that to her," Jonah laughs.

"Our nana doesn't have big ears." I feel another twinge

of guilt thinking about Nana, but I push it aside. "Anyway, the wolf says, 'The better to hear you with, my dear.' This goes on and on: 'What big eyes you have, Grandma'—'The better to see you with.' 'What big hands you have, Grandma'—'The better to hug you with.' And finally, Little Red Riding Hood says, 'My, Grandma, what big teeth you have.' And the wolf springs out of bed and says, 'The better to EAT you with!'" I bare my teeth for effect. "Then he gobbles up Little Red Riding Hood in seconds."

"Poor Grandma and Little Red Riding Hood!" Jonah cries. "I bet the wolf ate the cake, too. For dessert."

"Probably," I say. "Nothing like cake to wash down some people."

"Ew," Jonah laughs, but then his expression gets serious. "Then what happens?" he asks. "That can't be how it ends."

I think for a minute. "You know, there are actually TWO versions of the story, with two different endings. In the story by the Brothers Grimm, a hunter rushes in and cuts open the wolf's belly and out pops Grandma and Little Red Riding Hood. And they're totally okay."

"And how does the second version end?" Jonah asks, hugging Prince tight to him.

"Well . . ." I try to remember. "In the story by Charles Perrault, there is no hunter."

Jonah tilts his head. "No hunter? So who kills the wolf and saves Little Red Riding Hood and Grandma?"

I bite my lip again. "No one."

Jonah's eyes get big again. "Yikes. I like the Brothers Grimm one better."

I nod. "Me too."

"So . . . which version do you think we're in?"

"Snoooooort!"

I look over at the unconscious huntsman.

Oh! Oh! Oh! He's the hunter! Of course he's the hunter!

And if he's the hunter, then we're in the Grimm version. Woot! That's the good one!

"No worries, Jonah!" I say, relieved. "We're in the Grimm version. That's the hunter. Or huntsman. I'm not sure what the difference is."

"Um, Abby?"

"Yes, Jonah?"

"If that's the hunter, and he's unconscious . . ."

"Yeah?"

"Then who is going to save Little Red and her grandmother?"

"Snooooooort!"

"Oh," I say, my shoulders falling. "Crumbs."

chapter four

To Grandmother's House We Go

oes this mean I messed up the story when I fell on the hunter?" Jonah asks.

I nod. "It seems you did indeed mess up the story."

Jonah's cheeks flush. "So . . . what do we do now?"

Hmm. "I think we have to save Little Red," I say.

Jonah's eyes bug out. "You mean we have to cut open the wolf's belly to free Little Red and her nana?"

My stomach heaves. "Oh, I hope not. That's really, really gross. I was thinking more like we stop the wolf from eating them in the first place."

"Ah. Got it. That makes more sense. But how do we do that?" Jonah asks, frowning.

"I guess we go follow her," I say. I stand up and gaze down into the woods. I can still hear Little Red singing faintly in the distance.

"And leave the sleeping hunter?" Jonah asks, glancing back at the snoring man.

"Help is on the way, remember?" I say. "And we don't have time to wait for the doctor if we want to stop Little Red before the wolf gets her."

"Okay. I'm ready!" Jonah says. He leaps up with Prince in his arms, and heads for the ladder again.

"Wait!" I say, glancing at my wristwatch. "First we'd better figure out what time it is here." My watch keeps track of the time back home, which is helpful since time passes differently there than it does in fairy tale land. Time in some fairy tales goes faster than the time at home. Sometimes it goes slower. "Is there a clock?" I ask.

"There's one!" Jonah points at the clock on the hunts-man's desk. The time is 12:25. Since it's daylight outside, it must be 12:25 P.M.

I look down at my trusty watch again. 12:25 A.M. OH! Perfect. That means that time is passing at the same speed here as it is at home. And that we're exactly twelve hours ahead — or behind — here.

"We just have to get back home before Nana wakes up," Jonah says.

I swallow. After the fight we had, Nana would NOT be happy to find me missing in the morning.

No time to waste. "Let's go save Little Red!" I cry.

Jonah climbs down the ladder first with Prince in his arms. Then I go, stepping down, down, down carefully. The ladder sways. Eep. Finally, my feet hit the ground. Whew. I'm not the hugest fan of heights.

There's a horse tied up to the tree beside us. Must be the hunter's. He neighs at me and Jonah.

Then I hear a sound way off in the distance that makes all of us — including the horse — jump:

"Ah-ooooooooooooh!"

"What was *that*?" Jonah asks, his eyes huge. Prince bares his teeth and barks.

My heart is thumping hard. That sounded a lot like . . . a howl.

42

"Abby. Was that a wolf?" Jonah asks me, looking terrified.

"Um, probably not," I lie. Still, I can't hide my shiver. The howling came from somewhere to our left. Thankfully, we're going in the other direction — to catch up to Little Red.

"Come on," I tell Jonah, grabbing his arm and leading us away. Prince follows us closely. We don't hear any more howling, so I relax a little bit.

The forest path is a hard-packed dirt trail that winds through the enormous trees. Everywhere I look, there are more tree houses above us, in all different colors and shapes.

And I don't see any wolves. Yet.

"Abby, do you want to know something cool about wolves?" Jonah asks.

"Sure. Is it that they've now decided to become vegetarians?" I ask hopefully.

"No," Jonah says, stepping over a small rock.

"Is it that they are secretly scared of children?" I ask *extra* hopefully.

"Also no," Jonah says. "And you're making my thing sound less cool."

"Sorry, sorry, what is it?"

"It's that dogs came from wolves!" Jonah announces proudly.

Prince scampers alongside us. *Woof!*

"That's true," I agree, remembering what we learned in science class about animals. "Dogs are descended from wolves."

"So Prince's nana was a wolf," Jonah says.

I shake my head. "More like Prince's great-great-great-great-great-great-great-nana was a wolf. You'd have to go back a lot of generations in Prince's family to find a wolf."

Jonah bends down to scratch Prince behind the ears. "I wonder if wolves wag their tails when they're happy," Jonah says just as Prince wags *his* tail.

"I'm not sure I want to see a wolf happy," I say. "If a wolf is happy, we're probably not so happy."

As we come around a curve in the path, Jonah stops walking. He points ahead.

"Abby, there she is!" he whispers. "There's Super-Red!"

I see a red cloak billowing in the breeze.

Yay! We found her!

"Should we warn her about the wolf right now?" Jonah asks.

I hold a finger up to my lips. "Shhh," I say. "Let's just follow her quietly and see. We don't know exactly where she is in the story. Let's hope she hasn't met the wolf yet."

SNAP!

Oops. I just stepped on a twig.

"Way to be quiet," Jonah says.

Little Red Riding Hood turns around. She's wearing red sneakers that match her cape.

"Oh!" she says nervously, taking a big step back. "Hello."

"We didn't mean to scare you," I say.

"You didn't! It's just . . . there aren't that many kids in town," she explains.

Little Red looks to be a bit younger than I am, and a couple of inches shorter. She has brown skin, and dark brown bangs that fall into her eyes. The rest of her hair must be tucked up under the hood. She has huge light brown eyes and a dimple in each cheek when she finally smiles.

I smile back. "Hi!" I say, walking up to her. "I'm Abby

and this is my brother, Jonah. The dog sniffing your shoes is Prince."

Little Red kneels down and scratches Prince behind the ears. She seems less nervous now. "I LOVE dogs," she says. "I love all animals, really. They're so much easier to understand than people."

"What's *your* name?" Jonah asks her eagerly.

"Well, everyone calls me Little Red," she explains, gesturing to her red cloak. "But my real name is Lali. Which means 'red' in Hindi. That's why my grandmother made me this red cloak. To go with my name." She pauses and puts a hand to her lips. "Am I talking too much?"

"Not at all," Jonah says. "I talk A LOT. Plus, I *knew* you would have a color for a name!" he adds, giving me a smug smile.

"You did," I admit. Then I glance back at Little Red, aka Lali. "You mentioned your grandmother. Are you on your way to see her now?"

Lali looks surprised. "How do you know that?" she asks.

Jonah and I exchange a glance. "Just a lucky guess," I answer quickly.

"Yes, I'm going to my grandmother's cottage," Lali says. "But I was just about to stop to pick her some flowers." She points off the path to a little wooded patch where pretty wildflowers are growing.

"Flowers?" I ask, worried. "Why are you going to pick flowers?"

Lali straightens her hood. "I shouldn't show up at her house without flowers. At least that's what the wolf said. He suggested —"

AHHHHH! "You met the wolf?" I yell. Oh, no! "Did you tell him where your grandma's house is?"

She nods, looking confused. "I did. So what?" she asks.

"So what? SO WHAT?" I cry. "We have to get there immediately to save your grandmother!"

"We really do!" Jonah chimes in, and Prince barks.

Lali's eyes widen. "Uh-oh. Did I do something wrong? My grandmother says I'm always messing up!"

"Let's just go," I exclaim, taking Lali's arm. "What's the fastest way to your grandmother's house?"

"Well, I usually take the forest path, but I also know a shortcut —"

"Run!" I say, and we do.

Lali leads us on a shortcut through the trees. A few minutes later, huffing and puffing, Lali points to a tree cottage right above us.

"There it is!" Lali says, out of breath. "My grandmother's house."

This tree cottage is painted pale blue with white shutters. There are flower boxes in the windows and frilly lace curtains. A white ladder rests against the tree trunk, leading up to the doorway.

Lali takes a running leap onto the middle of the ladder, then scoots up two rungs at a time, her basket barely wobbling on her arm.

I look at Jonah. He's staring at her with his mouth hanging open.

"THAT. WAS. AWESOME!" he shouts, pumping his fist in the air. "Can you teach me how to do that?" he calls up to Lali.

"Oh, sure," she says, glancing back down with a shy

smile. "There's not much for me to do around here except get creative with ladder climbing."

Is it my imagination, or is Jonah staring at Little Red Riding Hood with dreamy eyes?

Lali leaps up to the small porch and opens the door.

"Little Red, please be careful . . ." I say.

"It's fine," she calls down. "Dadi — my grandma — is probably just sleeping."

What if the wolf got ahead of us? What if he gobbled up Lali's grandma, put on her sleeping cap, climbed into bed, and is just waiting to pounce?

I take a deep breath. We have to be brave. I climb up the ladder next, as fast as I can, Jonah and Prince behind me. The three of us follow Lali inside the cottage. My heart is pounding.

It's dark inside. The curtains are drawn, and I have to squint to see. There is a stone fireplace with a dying fire. Prince immediately curls up on the braided rug next to the fireplace and falls asleep. Our dog can nap anywhere. There's also a big overstuffed recliner and two smaller chairs in front of the fireplace. A white cane leans against one chair.

Across the room is a bed. And there's a lump in the bed! Someone is under the quilt!

I freeze.

Is it the grandma or the wolf?

Please be the grandma, please be the grandma.

"Little Red, is that you?" a very gruff voice calls from the bed.

"Don't answer," Jonah whispers to Lali. "It could be the wolf!"

I take a tiny step closer to the bed. No way am I getting TOO close.

I squint at the figure under the covers. I wish there was a light or a lantern — anything to help me see better.

Someone — something — is definitely under the quilt. And wearing a pink cap. I can see the neckline of a frilly lace bathrobe where the quilt is pulled up.

Is it Little Red's grandma?

Or the wolf in disguise?

Grandma?

Wolf?

Grandma?

Wolf?

Jonah pokes me with his elbow. "Abby, that *is* Little Red's grandmother, right?"

"Maybe?" I say.

"It's definitely my grandmother," Lali says. She takes off her hood and shakes out her long dark hair. "I know what Dadi looks like!"

"You call your grandma by her first name?" Jonah asks.

"'Dadi' is the Hindi word for my dad's mother," Lali explains. "But my dad passed away when I was two."

"I'm so sorry," I say.

"I said, is that YOU, Little Red?" the figure in the bed shouts, and slowly starts to sit up.

"I don't think that's the wolf," I whisper to Jonah. "The wolf was at least pretending to be nice in the story."

"Yeah," says Jonah.

"Look at the ears sticking out around the pink cap," I say, inching closer to the bed. "Way too small and round to be a wolf's ears. And look at the arms coming out from under the quilt. Not hairy at all!" Wolves are furry ALL over. Feeling more certain, I take another step closer. "And she doesn't have any teeth! This can't be the wolf."

"How dare you?" Dadi shouts at me, sitting up all the way and whipping off her sleeping cap.

I jump back, even though she's not the wolf.

Dadi is a lot older than Nana. She looks taller, too. She has brown eyes and brown skin like Little Red and the same dimples in each cheek, but her cheeks are thinner. Her black hair has some gray through it, and is up in a braided bun.

"She's definitely human," I say. She's still scary, though.

"You are the rudest children I have ever met!" Dadi bellows. "Of course I'm human! And I just don't have my dentures in! I wasn't expecting company!"

"But not having hairy arms is a compliment," Jonah points out.

Dadi leans forward and scowls at us. "You are *very* rude."

"I'm sorry," I say quickly. "We didn't mean it like that."

"You are a disgrace," she says.

Oof. I take another step back. So does Jonah. I glance at Lali and see that her shoulders are a bit slumped.

"Where's my muffin?" Dadi snaps at Lali. "BRING ME MY MUFFIN! And it better be good," she warns.

"Dadi, I think you're going to like the muffins today," Lali says, forcing a smile. "I made a batch this morning, and I put in extra blueberries like you like. Doesn't the smell make your mouth water?" Lali reaches into her basket and pulls out a blueberry muffin. She places it on a napkin and hands it to Dadi.

"Can she chew without teeth?" Jonah whispers to me.

"I have no idea," I say.

"You fools!" Dadi says to us. "I've been gumming muffins for years. But I *will* put in my dentures since you are being so rude about it."

She reaches into a glass of water on her nightstand, pops in a set of bright white teeth, and gives us a fake smile. Then she takes a bite of the muffin.

Dadi wrinkles her nose. "This muffin is overbaked!"

"It is?" Lali says, her face falling. "I'm sorry."

"Can I have one?" Jonah asks, practically batting his eyes at Lali.

"No, you cannot!" Dadi squawks. "Are *you* sick in bed?" She shakes her head. "The entitlement of kids today."

"What's entitlement?" Jonah asks me.

"It means you're all spoiled brats," Dadi says.

I glance at Lali. If she's bothered by her mean grandmother, she's not showing it. "Dadi, shall I heat up the muffin for you?" she offers.

"Humph!" Dadi says. "It'll just get even more over-baked." She eyes Little Red. "Come closer, girl."

Lali rushes over to the bed. "Yes, Dadi?"

"*What* is with that messy hair of yours?" Dadi demands. "And why is your cloak so wrinkled? How dare you come over here looking so sloppy? In my day, people dressed up nicely to see their elders."

"I'm sorry," Lali says again. "My cloak got tangled as I skipped. I'll iron it later. It'll be as smooth as the day you made it for me."

Dadi waves her hand dismissively. "And you two," she barks, staring at me and Jonah. "Why on earth are you in your pajamas in the middle of the day? Disgraceful!" She shakes her head. "Children are no-good nincompoops who can't do a thing right. Make messes all day long." She glances at Prince napping on the rug. "And just look at that lazy mutt!"

How dare she call Prince lazy! Or a mutt! Though I guess he is a mutt. I'll let that part slide.

"Would you like some tea, Dadi?" Little Red asks brightly. I think she's trying to change the subject. I hope it works.

"Of course I want tea," Dadi snaps. "Why would you ask such a silly question?"

"Dadi, I read in the *Howlton Gazette* the other day that keeping a positive outlook does wonders for your health." Lali takes the thermos out of her basket and pours out the hot tea into the lid-cup.

Dadi scowls. "Oh, hush with that ridiculous nonsense and give me my tea! It had better have just the amount of cream and sugar I like," she mutters.

"Of course it does, Dadi," Little Red says, carefully handing her grandma the cup.

"Well, I don't know how you could possibly know how I like my tea when you rarely visit me," Dadi grumbles. "You should come every day to bring me dessert and tea and fluff my pillow. But nooo, you only visit occasionally. And let's not even talk about my daughter-in-law, your mother. She never comes!"

Gee, I wonder why.

"Now, Dadi," Lali says, frowning. "You KNOW that Mom has to work. To make enough money to keep a roof over our heads and feed us."

"That is no excuse," Dadi says, taking another sip of tea. She scowls again. "You dawdled on the way over, didn't you?" she says accusingly, pointing a finger at Little Red. "This tea isn't hot enough!"

"Too hot would burn your lips," Lali says. "You know my mom and I want you to move in with us. If you did, your tea would always be piping hot. I could bring it to you straight from the kitchen to your bedroom in our house."

"Hush," Dadi says. "I will never leave my cottage! And you are horrible for asking me to." She shakes her head. "Overbaked muffins and lukewarm tea. Harrumph! Just what a dadi needs when she's ailing. What a bad grand-daughter you are!"

Lali hangs her head, but she rushes over to the bed to fluff Dadi's pillows anyway. I feel awful for her.

"Poor Lali," I whisper to Jonah.

"Yeah," Jonah whispers back. "She doesn't deserve this. She's so sweet."

Is Jonah blushing? Yes! His cheeks are pink. I can practically see cartoon hearts shooting out of his scrawny chest as he sneaks another peek at Lali. I think Jonah has his first crush!

"Dadi is horrible," Jonah adds.

"With a capital H," I whisper back.

"She's making me wish we hadn't saved her," he says.

"Jonah!" I admonish him.

"I'm kidding. Kind of. We're so lucky that our nana is so great," Jonah adds thoughtfully. "She's always nice to us."

I nod, feeling a little lump in my throat as I remember the fight I had with Nana.

Suddenly, there's a loud banging on the door.

Knock-knock! KNOCK!

My back stiffens.

KNOCK KNOCK KNOCK.

AHHHHH!

I know who that is.

The wolf is here!

chapter five

Knock Knock. Who's There?

now who is it?" Dadi demands. "Lali, go see who's at the door."

"NO!" I cry. "Don't!"

Dadi and Lali stare at me.

"Um, I mean, I think it might be the wolf," I explain.

"The wolf?" Dadi asks. "Which one? There's a whole family of wolves in Howlton." She guffaws. "And as if wolves can climb ladders. Hahaha. Pajama Girl thinks wolves can walk up ladders. Good one. Or are you just not that bright?"

"Hey!" Jonah says with a scowl. "My sister is very smart."

Why thank you, Jonah. I do happen to be an excellent thinker, even under pressure.

But while we're on the subject, wolves *can't* climb ladders? I really, really hope that's true. Except the wolf ate Grandma and Little Red in the original story. So obviously wolves CAN climb ladders. At least some of them can.

Knock-knock-KNOCK!

The knocking wakes Prince and he scrambles up with a worried bark.

"What Dadi means," Lali explains, "is that the reason everyone in Howlton lives in tree houses is because wolves can't climb trees or ladders."

Oh. Well, I guess that explains the whole tree house thing. But Lali must be wrong because I know the way the story goes. Or at least the way it's supposed to go.

"Don't speak for me!" Dadi hollers.

Knock-knock! Knock-knock!

"Look," I say, lowering my voice. "I *know* it's the wolf — er, *a* wolf," I correct myself. "Just trust me."

Lali nods. "If my new friend Abby says it's a wolf, then I believe her."

I smile at Lali. She really is so sweet.

Dadi rolls her eyes. "You'll trust anyone! Foolish girl!"

"My sister knows what she's talking about," Jonah argues. "Hide, everyone!"

The banging on the door gets louder.

Dadi scrunches up her face. "Although . . . it's true that no one comes to visit me but Little Red. And she's here. Maybe it IS a wolf!"

We all hurry to different hiding spots. Lali helps Dadi out of bed and leads her to the closet. They huddle inside and shut the door. Jonah and I duck behind the overstuffed chair. And Prince flees under the bed.

I hold a finger up to my lips. "Shhh," I whisper to Jonah.

"I wish Little Red were over here with us and not with her grandma," Jonah whispers.

Me too. I mean, I know Jonah has a little crush on Lali, but even I wouldn't be surprised if Dadi hid behind Little Red to save herself from the wolf.

I'm about to respond when I hear a weird sound. Like

wood tinkering. Oh my goodness. The wolf is picking the lock with a twig!

I stare at the doorknob. Which suddenly and slowly turns . . .

The wolf is about to break in!

The door creaks open.

CREAK. It's pushed open even wider.

And someone bursts in!

I gasp.

It's not the wolf.

It's . . . Nana?

chapter six

The Grandmother of All Surprises

ana!" Jonah exclaims, and goes rushing out from our hiding spot. He flings himself at our grandmother and throws his arms around her.

"Jonah!" Nana cries, hugging him back. "You're okay! Where's Abby?"

I come out of the hiding spot, still in shock.

"Right here," I say, blinking very slowly. "But . . . how? How are you possibly here?"

"I'm so glad you're both all right," Nana says, hurrying over to give me a hug. I hug her, too, forgetting all about our fight for the time being. There are more pressing matters to deal with. LIKE WHY IS NANA HERE, INSIDE A FAIRY TALE?

Prince scampers out from under the bed and jumps up on Nana's legs, barking happily and wagging his tail.

Little Red and Dadi emerge from the closet, and they stare at Nana in surprise.

"Hello!" Nana says to them. "I'm Abby and Jonah's nana. You must be Little Red Riding Hood and Little Red Riding Hood's grandmother."

HOW DOES SHE KNOW THAT? WHAT IS HAPPENING?

Lali nods shyly. "Yes, hello," she says politely. "I'm Little Red, but my real name is Lali." She shakes Nana's hand.

"It's a pleasure to meet you," Nana says to her. "I've heard so much about you!"

"You've heard about me?" Lali asks. "From who?"

Nana thinks for a second. "Um, just around. I love your cape."

"Ah," Lali says. "It does kind of set me apart. Everyone knows that when they see a red cape, it's me!" She does a cartwheel right in the middle of the tree cottage, her cape billowing around her.

Dadi lifts her chin. "I got out of bed for nothing!" she snaps. "You" — she points at me — "said a wolf was at the door!" She climbs back into her bed and pulls the quilt up to her chin. "I am taking a nap. You have exhausted me."

She angrily lowers a sleep mask over her eyes and turns onto her side.

"Isn't she glad Abby was wrong?" Jonah asks. "I definitely am. Great to see you, Nana!"

"Great to see you, too," Nana says.

"But . . . but . . ." I sputter. I have so many questions, I don't even know where to start. Finally, I just exclaim, "HOW ARE YOU HERE?"

"Maybe we should have a little chat," Nana suggests. She gestures to the overstuffed chair by the fireplace. "Is it all right if we sit down?" she asks Lali.

"Of course," Lali says. "In the meantime, I'll prepare some snacks for you guys." She picks up her basket and disappears into the kitchen.

"She's so cool," Jonah says, watching Lali go.

Nana sits down in the overstuffed chair, and Jonah and I sit in the two smaller chairs. Prince curls up on the rug and is asleep again within seconds.

"Nana," I say. "You seem to know where we are. Do you?"

I can't even imagine how confused our nana must have been this whole time. I mean, one minute, she's in our basement around midnight for reasons I still don't know. The next, she's sucked through a magic mirror into another world. A fairy tale world!

Nana smiles and nods at me. "Oh, I know exactly where we are, Abby."

I tilt my head and stare at Nana. "You do?" Huh? How?

"We're in the story of *Little Red Riding Hood*!" she responds.

"But how do you know we're in Little Red Riding Hood's story?" I ask, my mind exploding.

Lali comes back in the room, holding a tray with four glasses of lemonade. She sets the tray down on the end table. "I have a story?" she asks.

Nana gives Lali a nod and a smile. "You sure do."

"Must be because of my cape," Lali says, heading back into the kitchen. "I'm going to warm up the muffins and bring some out."

"Thank you, Lali!" Jonah calls after her, blushing again.

"But, Nana," I say, "how did you even get here?"

"I know a portal when I see one!" Nana explains.

Okay. WHAT? This isn't making sense.

I stare at her. My little old nana in her pink pj's with the little white clouds on them and her fuzzy orange slippers.

"Nana, how could you possibly know about portals?" I ask.

She takes a deep breath. "Because I had one as a kid."

Wait, WHAT? Did she just say that?

Did I hear that right?

Jonah jumps in his seat. "You had a magic mirror just like us?" he asks.

"Not a magic *mirror*," Nana says. "But I'll get to what mine was. First let me start with tonight."

Good. Because I'm seriously confused. None of this makes sense. I don't like things that make no sense!

Nana takes a sip of her lemonade, then sets the glass down. "I was fast asleep, but something woke me up — noises that I realized were coming from the basement. I think I heard your voice, Abby, saying, 'Do not come.' I had no idea what you were talking about, so I hurried downstairs. I didn't see you guys, but I did see the mirror swirling purple."

"I was telling Jonah not to follow me," I admit, giving Jonah a smile. "Which I am glad he ignored."

"So am I," Nana says.

"Did you jump through the mirror right away?" Jonah asks Nana.

"Well, I thought about it for a minute," Nana says. "I figured you two had been to stories before without a grown-up. But I'm responsible for you while your parents are away. I couldn't just let you go alone. So yes, I jumped through."

"I can't believe this," I say. My mouth is so parched from shock that I take a sip of my lemonade. "You had a magic portal? It took you to fairy tales?"

Nana nods, her gray curls bouncing. "It did. Just a few. When I was a young girl living in Toronto, Canada, I discovered that my closet door was magical. Sometimes, when I opened it, I could step through it into stories. But not all the time."

"A closet portal?" I cry. "Amazing!"

"It was," Nana says happily.

"Which stories have you been to?" Jonah asks.

"Let's see," Nana says, rubbing her chin. "*Snow White. The Little Mermaid. Jack and the Beanstalk*. And now, *Little Red Riding Hood*."

Jonah's mouth drops open. "YOU'VE been to *Jack and the Beanstalk*? I'm dying to go! That's my favorite story."

Nana smiles. "I'm sure one day you will go, too. And you'll do great things, just as you always have in stories. Unlike me."

I tilt my head. "What do you mean?"

"I was pretty timid as a kid and never changed anything in the stories," Nana explains. "I never made things better for anyone or stopped the bad guys. I was too scared. I hid behind trees or crowds at the castle and watched. But it seems like you guys do things a little differently."

"We do!" I say. "We get right in there. Usually by accident."

"Sometimes on purpose," Jonah says.

"Wait," I say, glancing back at Nana. "How do you know that we do great things in stories?"

"Maryrose told me," Nana says.

I gasp. "You met Maryrose?"

Nana nods. "She appeared in the mirror just as I was about to jump through. She assured me that you two would be fine, but she understood if I wanted to check for myself. We chatted for a while."

"Did you have a Maryrose, too?" I ask. "In your closet?"

"No," Nana says a little sadly. "There was no fairy who ever spoke to me."

"Did the portal move with you when you moved to America?" I ask.

Nana shakes her head. "After my parents moved us to Chicago, I never found another portal. I kept searching, though. Even after I grew up and got married and had your mom, I knocked on everything. Windows! Mirrors! Closet doors! Back doors! But nothing ever swirled or turned purple. In time, I started to wonder if I had dreamed the whole thing — going into stories. But then, tonight, I saw the mirror in the basement of your house and I just *knew*."

"Wow," I say.

"Is it strange that I'm here with you?" Nana asks.

"Yeah," I say. "But also pretty great."

I study Nana. For a second, I can see myself in her.

I mean, we have very similar eyes and the same nose, now that I'm looking. And her hair is curly like mine.

I never realized how much I look like my nana. And now we have something else in common. Something HUGE.

My nana had a magic closet door! She went into fairy tales! I have a magic mirror! I go into fairy tales!

"I'm still so amazed," I say. "You really had a magic portal as a kid."

"I really did," she says. "I wish I'd had a Maryrose, too."

"Yeah," I say. "But then again, poor Maryrose is trapped in our mirror."

"Oh, right," Nana says.

"That's one of the reasons she keeps sending us into stories," I explain. "She wants us to figure out how to free her." I pause, thinking. "I wonder why *you* got to go into stories."

"Maybe there was a fairy trapped in your portal, too," Jonah says to Nana. "Maryrose didn't speak to us right away. Maybe your fairy was shy."

"That's possible," Nana says. "I was shy, too. But Maryrose was very kind."

I smile at the idea of Nana and Maryrose chatting. "No wonder you didn't fall into the huntsman's tree house right after us," I say. "Maryrose probably kept the portal open while you two talked."

"Exactly," Nana says. "I was a little worried when I arrived inside the tree house and you two were already gone. Also, there was a man sleeping on the floor."

"He was unconscious," Jonah says, looking sheepish. "I landed on him."

"Oh, dear," Nana says worriedly.

"We called the doctor," I say quickly.

"Good thinking," Nana says. "Well, I looked out the door, saw you two on the path, and climbed down the ladder to follow you."

"You did?" I ask. "We didn't notice!"

She nods. "I'm pretty good at being sneaky."

"Wow," I say again.

"Well, we're really glad you're here," Jonah says.

"I bet you're not glad that I'M here," a deep voice snarls.

We all whirl around.

There, at the open door, is a big silver wolf with a white snout.

AHHHH!

chapter seven

A Wolf in the House

For a second, all I can do is stare. This wolf isn't like any wolf I've ever seen. Not that I've ever seen a wolf this close up. But I was expecting a big, furry, vicious-looking animal on all fours.

That is NOT what is standing in the doorway.

And yes, I mean standing. The wolf is on two legs like a person!

He's also wearing a concert T-shirt and blue shorts. And is that a macramé bracelet on his left ankle? I think it is. Great. He can be in the anklet club with Penny and my friends.

He has silver-gray fur and a white chest. His eyes are a yellow-gold. And he's a little on the skinny side. But standing up the way he is, he's at least six feet tall.

His teeth are very, very sharp. I know because he's baring them at us as he snarls.

"Which one of you should I eat first?" the wolf asks.

My heart leaps. This is not good. Not good at all.

The wolf looks around at all of us. Me. Nana. Jonah. Prince, who's just woken up with a loud bark. Little Red, who's now standing in the room, holding the tray of muffins. And Dadi, still asleep in her bed. How is she sleeping through this?

The wolf licks his lips. His long pink tongue — as long as Prince's tail! — is hanging over his huge, pointy fangs.

My knees feel weak.

Prince gets up and pads carefully over to the wolf. He doesn't come too close, though. He flattens his floppy ears, lowers his head, and lets out a low growl.

"Grr! Grr!"

"Hahaha!" the wolf says to Prince. "You're SO scary!"

Prince barks and takes a few steps backward, but stays between us and the wolf, like he's protecting us.

"Hey," Lali says, "you're the wolf I ran into on the forest path! You told me to pick flowers for my grandma!"

The wolf darts his golden eyes over to her. "That's me," he says proudly.

"You tricked me!" Lali says.

"You were easy to trick," he says. "You were so eager to please your grandmother that you didn't realize I was just trying to stall you!"

Lali's shoulders fall. "You're right."

The wolf snarls in delight.

"I have a question," Jonah asks.

Seriously? A question? Right now?

"What?" The wolf shivers and rubs his furry silver arms.

"I thought wolves couldn't climb ladders," Jonah says. "How did you get up here?"

The wolf snickers. "Actually, I learned by watching Lali."

"Me?" Lali asks, surprised.

"Yes! For a while now, I've been hiding in the forest. I've studied how you take your running leaps onto the ladder and climb up two by two with one hand."

Lali cocks her head to one side. "I'm not sure if I should be flattered."

"It took me forever to learn," the wolf continues. "I found an abandoned tree house outside of town, and I've been practicing. But I kept slipping down. Stupid slippery paws," he adds, kicking up a foot. "But eventually, I could get myself up. Not anywhere as fast as you, of course."

"She's amazing," Jonah whispers to me, smiling all moony again, despite the fact that a wolf is about to eat us all.

We need to escape. *Or* we need to trap him. Yeah, that sounds a bit more doable. But how? Maybe I should keep him talking for now and hope someone else figures something out.

"I have another question," I say.

"Now what?" the wolf asks, narrowing his eyes on me.

"Um . . . um . . . Is Poptastic a band?" I ask, pointing at the logo on his T-shirt. "What do they play?"

"They're the best band in Howlton," the wolf says. "They play all kinds of songs." He shivers again. He seems kind of cold. And he's awfully skinny.

Out of the corner of my eye, I see Nana moving backward. Her gaze is on the wolf but her hand is reaching behind her.

Oh, good! Does she have a plan? Please, please, please let her have a plan.

As the wolf continues talking about Poptastic, Nana grabs Dadi's frilly lace bathrobe from the chair beside the bed. Then, with the robe behind her back, Nana moves toward the wolf.

This is part of a plan, right? Please, please, please let it be part of a plan.

The wolf rubs his chin and then names a few songs. "Wait, I changed my mind. I think 'Moonbeam' is also in my top five." He shivers again.

"Are you cold?" Nana asks the wolf. "Why don't you put this on?" she offers, holding out the bathrobe.

He sneers at the yellow robe. "I don't need that." Then he pauses. "Well . . . I guess it is pretty chilly. Oh, maybe for a minute."

"Here, let me help," Nana says, stepping toward him with the robe. "I am a nana, after all."

"Fine," the wolf says.

Nana holds out the robe with the opening facing the wolf. "Just put your arms through here," she says.

I realize she's putting the robe on him backward, like it's a hospital robe. Why would she do that? The back of the robe is on his front and the sleeves are facing behind him.

"And now just let me tie the belt so you'll be nice and toasty."

Before the wolf can even blink, Nana has the sleeves of the robe tied together behind his back. And the belt wrapped twice and hooked to the doorknob!

He's trapped!

It *was* a plan!

Nana had a plan!

Hurrah!

"Hey!" he growls, baring his pointy teeth.

Nana grabs a pearl necklace off the dresser, tosses it around his neck, and laces it around a hook.

"Go, Nana!" I say, high-fiving her. How awesome is she? I mean, I knew she was amazing, even if I was mad at her. Even if I'm still a little mad at her. But I didn't know she was this gutsy!

Didn't Nana say she was a timid kid? She definitely grew out of that.

"Hey!" the wolf shouts again. "How dare you? Let me go this minute!"

"No way," Nana says. "You're not eating anyone in this tree cottage, do you hear me, wolf?"

Instead of snarling or baring his teeth again, the wolf does something kind of shocking.

He bursts into tears.

Huge sobs come out of his mouth. Tears roll down his furry cheeks.

WHAT? Jonah and I glance at each other in surprise.

"Does anyone have a tissue?" the wolf asks, another sob wrenching from his throat.

Lali picks up the box of tissues from Dadi's bedside table and brings a tissue over to the wolf.

"Not too close, Lali," I warn her. "It's probably a trick."

She hesitates. Then she dabs the tissue under the wolf's eyes and then holds it under his nose for him to blow. He does.

"Thanks," the wolf says.

"No problem," Lali answers.

"You guys just don't understand," the wolf says, blinking away his tears. "I'm so hungry and cold, and my family is mean to me, and that horrible hunter has been chasing me for years."

Too bad the hunter didn't chase him over here. We could use a hunter right about now.

The wolf sniffles. "I don't even like eating people."

Yeah, right.

"What *do* you like to eat?" Jonah asks.

"Burgers. Hot dogs. I like people food, not people." The wolf looks around at all of us. "Please untie me. Please! Pretty please?"

Lali glances over at me. "What do you think, Abby?"

"I think he's tricking us," I say.

"I'm not tricking you, I swear!" the wolf huffs.

I'm still suspicious. "You say that, but I know how this story goes," I tell the wolf. "I know you were going to eat Little Red and her grandma!"

"I . . . I . . . okay, I was!" he says, pouting. "But only because I'm really hungry! There is not a lot of food in Howlton. I had no choice. So I finally learned how to climb

79

ladders to get some food . . . and now you're making me feel bad about planning to eat you!"

"Um, sorry?" I say.

"What's your name?" Jonah asks the wolf.

"Owen," he says.

Owen? I was expecting something like Brutus or Killer or Thor.

But now that I know the wolf a little, maybe not.

Owen starts crying again. "What am I going to do NOW?" he wails. "Hungry, hunted — and trust me, if you met my sister, you'd feel even worse for me."

"Is she mean?" Lali asks.

"The meanest," Owen says. "If you see a pure-white wolf with glowing gold eyes, run."

Now we all shiver.

"Thanks for the tip," Nana says.

"Can we get you something to eat?" Lali asks. "Something besides us? Some muffins, maybe?"

He nods. "That would be nice."

"So you *really* don't like eating humans?" I ask, stepping closer to him.

"I really don't. You're not that tasty. You need *a lot* of salt. Like a bucket-load."

"Have you tried dipping us in ketchup?" Jonah asks.

"Don't give him any ideas," I say, nudging my brother in the ribs.

"Listen, I promise I won't eat you," the wolf says. "Promise, promise, promise. And now I like you guys. I could never eat people I like!"

I look him in the eyes. "You're not going to eat us if we let you go? Swear?"

"I double-decker swear," Owen says.

I turn to Nana. "What do you think?"

She nods. "We can untie him," Nana says. "But I'm watching you," she tells the wolf. "Any funny business and we'll never trust you again. Got it?"

"Got it," he says gravely. "No funny business. You have my word."

Nana unties him and unhooks the necklace. Then Owen steps inside and Nana shuts the door.

"Thank you," Owen says, accepting a blueberry muffin from Lali and taking a bite. "You're all very kind."

"What is going on here?" Dadi asks, sitting up in her bed. She reaches for her glasses and puts them on. "Have my eyes gotten worse or is there a wolf in my cottage eating a muffin?"

"There is a wolf in your cottage eating a muffin," Jonah says.

"But he's a nice wolf," Lali adds. "Maybe."

"Can I have some lemonade?" Owen asks. "I'm parched."

Greedy, isn't he?

"Sure," Lali says, heading into the kitchen.

Woof! Prince barks, stepping over to sniff the wolf's foot.

"Hi there, little fellow," Owen says. "Sorry if I scared you before." He kneels down to pet him. "You're one of us. Sort of."

Prince's ears perk up and then his tail wags. Wow. Owen passed the Prince test.

Lali returns from the kitchen and gives Owen a glass of lemonade, which he swallows down in one big gulp.

"Thanks," Owen says. At least he has manners.

"Now that our *guest* is no longer parched," Dadi says, "I need you to run my bath, Lali. That's part of the reason you come to visit me, isn't it? To help me? Not just to chat with your friends?"

"Yes, Dadi," Lali says, looking down.

"Can't Nana help instead?" Jonah asks, clearly wanting to spend more time with Lali.

Nana smiles and gets to her feet. "I'd be happy to. Come along, now," she says. She walks over to Dadi, helping her out of bed.

Jonah turns to Lali and blushes. "So, Lali. Do you have . . . um . . . a favorite color?"

She shrugs. "Red, I guess?"

He blushes again. "Oh. Right. Of course. Do you like ketchup? That's red."

She nods. "I do."

"Me too!" he says excitedly.

Oh, brother.

"Personally," Owen says, "I'm more of a mustard fan. Have you ever put mustard on roasted potatoes?" He smacks his lips. "Once, I found a whole plate of potatoes outside someone's tree house and they were delicious."

"My nana makes great roasted potatoes," I say. "I bet she could give you the recipe."

"If only I had my own stove," Owen says. "We have no stove in our den."

"Where's your den?" I ask. "And who's 'we'?"

"I live with my siblings in a cave, just outside of town," Owen explains. "My sister is Tina, and my brothers are Thurston and Harley. I'm the youngest." He sighs. "They're always bossing me around. They think they know everything. And they would never let me make potatoes. They don't like eating people food. They like eating people."

I shiver again.

"I try to make them happy," Owen continues sadly. "I learned to climb ladders! But they're always criticizing me. I'm too slow. I'm too sensitive. I'm never enough, you know?" His eyes tear up.

"Oh, I know," Lali pipes up.

I look back and forth between them. Who knew Lali and the wolf would have something in common?

Knock-knock! Knock!

Someone else is pounding on the door.

"Who could that be?" I ask.

"Not sure," the wolf says.

"What if it's your sister?" Lali asks Owen, her eyes growing big.

Uh-oh.

Here we go again.

chapter eight

What Big Eyes I Have

Jonah, Lali, and Prince run off to hide in the kitchen.

I'm about to follow them, but Owen stops me.

"No way it's my sister," Owen says. "She definitely can't climb ladders."

KNOCK-KNOCK-KNOCK!

"Then who could it be?" I hiss.

The wolf's face pales. "Oh, no! It's probably the hunter!"

"It can't be," I say. "Jonah landed on him."

"Huh?" Owen asks.

"It's a long story," I say. "But he's unconscious. At least, he was unconscious."

"Hello?" a deep voice bellows from outside. "Is anyone there?"

"It sounds like the hunter," Owen says, trembling.

"Well . . . We called for a doctor," I admit.

"What?" Owen cries. "Why would you do that?"

"Because he was unconscious!"

"Good! It's better if he's unconscious!"

"Owen!" I say. "Just hide, okay?"

"Where?"

"I don't know. Under the bed?"

Owen leaps beneath the bed skirt and squeezes himself under the bed. "It's not exactly roomy under here," he complains.

"Just do it," I say.

"Don't tell the hunter I'm here!" Owen begs from beneath the bed. "Please! You need to pretend to be Little Red's grandma and tell him everything's okay or else he'll search the house!"

"I don't need to pretend —" I start, but then I pause.

I do need to pretend. The hunter SAW me in his house — right before Jonah knocked him out. I don't want the hunter to recognize me. He might get pretty mad.

I guess I *do* have to dress up as Dadi!

KNOCK-KNOCK-KNOCK.

"One second!" I holler.

I rush over to where Owen left the bathrobe, and I put it on over my pajamas. Then I grab the pink nightcap from the bedside table and slap it on my head. It actually does feel like a shower cap. Why would anyone sleep in this? I have no idea. I pull it as low around my face as I can. And then I jump into the bed and yank the covers up high. I grab Dadi's reading glasses from the nightstand and put those on, too. I hear water running in the bathroom. Hopefully Nana and Dadi won't hear anything.

Knock-knock-KNOCK!

"Come in," I call, my voice shaking. The glasses make everything look blurry and ginormous. They are already giving me a headache.

The door bursts open and a man comes in. He's very tall with a shock of bright red hair and a scruffy beard. He's wearing a green vest with a case of arrows strung across his torso and he is holding a bow in one hand. Yup, definitely the hunter. Or huntsman. Whatever. Definitely the guy Jonah landed on.

Also, Dadi's glasses make him look massive. These things really work.

"Is that you, Dadi?" the huntsman asks me.

"Yes," I croak out, trying to sound old and grumpy. I need to get into character! "What do you want? Why are you disturbing me?" I bark.

"I'm looking for a silver wolf with a white snout. He's probably wearing a concert T-shirt. Have you seen him sneaking around?"

"No, sonny," I say. "I haven't seen a wolf."

I notice that the huntsman has a red welt on his forehead. Probably from when Jonah accidentally clobbered him.

"Are you okay?" I ask, pointing to his head.

"I was attacked," the huntsman says. "By a young girl and her accomplices! I woke up just in time to see one of the intruders running from my tree house!"

"Really?" I say, trying to hide my fear. He saw us leaving his tree house? Yikes. I'm so glad he didn't catch us! "But you're okay?" I ask. "The doctor helped?"

"What doctor?" he asks. "I didn't see a doctor."

Maybe the doctor got there after the hunter had already left. At least the hunter's okay.

The hunter is still standing near the door. He better stay near the door. Otherwise he's going to notice that I'm not exactly a senior citizen. I could use some wrinkles made out of Play-Doh or something. Next time.

"This wolf is a crafty one," the huntsman says. "He climbs ladders! But don't worry. I'm going to get him. I'm going to get all the wolves, one by one. And then I'm going to hang them on my wall!"

"Oh, my," I say.

I hear a sob come from under the bed. Is Owen crying again? Oh, no! The hunter will hear!

I look down and the bed skirt is shaking.

Crumbs, crumbs, crumbs.

The hunter slides his gaze over to where mine is. I quickly look away.

"Why is there a paw sticking out from under your bed?" the hunter asks.

"There isn't!" I say. "Definitely not. That's just the . . . foot of the bed."

"Why is it hairy?"

"To keep it warm," I say. "Go away!"

The hunter stalks over and lifts up the bed skirt.

"Ahhh!" Owen shrieks.

But before Owen can even defend himself, the hunter points an arrow at him and shoots him in the foot.

Owen squawks and then goes quiet. Oh, no!

"You killed him!" I yell, jumping out of bed.

"I did not!" the huntsman says. "I just put him to sleep." He rubs his hands together. "It will be easier to kill him back at my tree house. With the sun setting through the windows, it's the perfect way to spend an evening! Murder at sunset! It's the best."

That is so, so, so creepy.

The hunter grabs Owen by the foot and pulls him out from under the bed. Owen's out cold. But at least he's alive.

"No!" I tell the huntsman. "You can't."

"Why not?" the huntsman asks. "He's a wolf! I've been hunting this one for years. I want his head on my tree house wall. I have no wolves . . . yet."

"Don't take him!" I call out. "Jonah! Lali! Prince! Help!"

The hunter throws a limp Owen over his shoulder and heads for the door.

Prince races out from the kitchen and lunges for the hunter's leg, grabbing on with his teeth.

"Beat it, mutt!" the hunter says, shaking Prince off him.

Jonah tries to grab the hunter's arm, but the hunter aims his arrow at Jonah.

"Don't you dare!" I cry, jumping in front of Jonah.

"You people better leave me alone or you'll be next!" the hunter threatens.

"You wouldn't hurt humans," Lali says, crossing her arms tightly. "Would you?"

"I will hurt whoever gets in my way," the hunter says. Then he throws open the door, Owen still slumped over his shoulder. "You should be thanking me! I am saving you from the wolf!"

Jonah, Lali, Prince, and I rush to the door as the hunter carries Owen down the ladder. We watch as the hunter drapes Owen on the back of his horse, then hops on in front of him and gallops away.

Clomp-clomp. Clomp-clomp. The hunter rides fast along the forest path, disappearing through the enormous trees.

"What do we do now?" Jonah asks.

"I don't know," I say.

"This was kind of how the story was supposed to go . . ." Jonah says. "You know? The hunter gets the wolf. That's the *happy* ending."

"It doesn't feel so happy," I say. There's a lump in my throat. "Poor Owen."

"Happy ending?" Lali cries. "You call that a happy ending? Owen was just wolf-napped! Why are you just standing there? We have to save him!"

"Yeah," Jonah says. His eyes light up. "YEAH! We have to save him, Abby!"

"Okay," I say. "We'll save Owen."

The bathroom door creaks open and Nana and Dadi step out.

"What is all the ruckus out here?" Dadi asks, wrapped in a big fluffy towel. "And excuse me, Pajama Girl, I do not remember giving you permission to wear my bathrobe, cap, and glasses."

Oops.

chapter nine

All in the Family

We're going to save Owen!" Lali announces, hands on her hips. "Who's coming?"

"I'll come," Nana offers.

"Yeah. Let's go, team!" Jonah cries. "Team Lali! I mean, team us!"

"You're leaving already?" Dadi snorts. "Figures." She gets back into bed.

"I'll come back later," Lali tells her grandmother. "Promise."

Dadi narrows her eyes. "Don't do me any favors."

"We have to save Owen before sunset," I say. "That's when the hunter said he was going to kill him. Lali, do you know what time the sun goes down here?"

"Around six," she says.

I look at my watch. "It's three thirty now. So we have a few hours before sunset. What's our plan?"

"Perhaps we should call the police," Nana says.

"But it's not a crime to hunt wild animals in Howlton," Lali says. "So the police won't do much."

"I called the help line earlier," I say. "When Jonah landed on the huntsman. I don't know if the doctor ever made it to his cottage, though. Maybe the doctor will show up now and stop the huntsman from hurting Owen?"

"You called Mona?" Lali asks.

"Yes," I say. "How do you know Mona?"

"Everyone knows Mona!" Lali says. "She's the town help line. She's the doctor *and* the policewoman *and* the firewoman!"

"She's all three?" Jonah asks.

"Yup."

"I guess that's why she's slow," I say.

"She can get super busy," Lali admits.

Nana clears her throat. "Why don't I head over to the hunter's tree house? Maybe I'll be able to reason with him. Grown-up to grown-up."

"You're not going by yourself," I say. "It could be really dangerous."

"I'm perfectly capable of handling dangerous situations, Abby," Nana huffs.

"Fairy tales are tricky," I say. "Once you mess them up . . . you never know what can happen. We're not letting you go anywhere alone."

"Then we'll all go together," Nana says.

"Okay," I agree, looking at Jonah and Lali. They nod. Prince barks.

We say good-bye to Dadi, and she grunts in return. Then the four of us take turns climbing down the ladder — I carry Prince — and we're on our way.

We are only a few minutes down the path when we hear:
AH-OOOH! AH-OOOOOOH!

It's the howling sound Jonah and I heard before. And it's coming from deep in the woods.

"Those are wolves, right?" I ask.

Breathe, Abby, breathe.

"Yup," Lali responds.

Jonah and I exchange a frightened glance.

"I knew it!" Jonah cries. "We heard the howling earlier."

Nana immediately pulls Jonah close to her, shielding him with her arms. "I'll keep you safe, sweetie," she tells him.

"I'm okay, Nana," Jonah argues, stepping away from her and blushing as he glances at Little Red.

Aw. NOW Jonah's embarrassed by Nana's hugs!

"Did you know that's why the town is called Howlton?" Lali asks. "'Cause of all the howling."

"Oh," I say. Since Owen isn't exactly in howl mode at the moment, that means . . .

. . . HIS FAMILY IS OUT THERE.

Including his evil sister.

AH-OOOH! AH-OOOOOOH!

"We need to hide," Nana says.

"But where?" I ask.

She motions to an enormous tree trunk. We all duck behind it. Prince lies down and covers his eyes with his paws.

The howling seems to be coming from farther down the path. I peek out from behind the tree to look. I don't see anything.

Ah-ooh! Ah-oooooh!

I grab a fallen branch off the ground and push Jonah behind me. I hold the big stick out in front of me.

Nana nods and grabs a stick, too. So do Jonah and Lali. Prince picks up a skinny branch in his mouth.

The howling continues. *AH-OOH! AH-OOH!*

"Tell me it's my imagination that it's getting closer?" I say.

"It's not your imagination," Jonah says. "It's definitely getting closer."

And then —

"Wolf!" Jonah cries, pointing.

I glance to the left. A bright white wolf with cold, golden eyes is standing and staring at the five of us. She's wearing a black leather jacket, dark-wash jeans, and has a rhinestone-dotted bow clipped to her furry left ear.

Wolves kind of have awesome accessories.

But still. AHHHH!

"That must be Tina," Lali whispers.

"Well, well," Tina says. "Five delicious-looking snacks."

She glances at each one of us and licks her lips. Then she turns to glance behind her. "Where are those nincompoop brothers of mine?" She shakes her head. "Thurston! Harley! Over here!"

While her back is turned, I mouth *RUN* to Jonah, Nana, Lali, and Prince. The five us turn to flee.

As we're dashing off, I spot the two wolf brothers hurrying over to Tina — one is incredibly tall, and one is super short, like my size.

"NO!" I hear Tina yell at them. "They're getting away, you fools!"

"Sorry," the taller wolf says. "I had to go to the bathroom."

"Idiots!" she screeches.

Nana, Jonah, Lali, Prince, and I all run for our lives for a good quarter mile. We take cover again behind a huge tree, catching our breaths.

I can see the three wolves running toward us. Oh no. Oh no. Oh no.

But they run right past our tree. Phew.

"I think they went this way!" I hear Tina call to her brothers. "I see footprints on the path!"

Now they're running in the opposite direction.

"They're following our footprints back to Dadi's!" Lali whispers. "Is my dadi safe?" she asks worriedly.

"Wolves can't climb ladders," I remind her. "Except for Owen, of course."

Ah-ooh! Ah-ooh!

Now the sound is getting closer. As if they're circling back to find us!

I glance up and see a tree house ahead. A really, really big one. "Let's head for that tree house!" I say, pointing. "The wolves won't be able to climb the ladder. We can stay there until they're gone."

"Good idea!" Nana says. "Do you know who lives here?" she asks Lali.

Lali nods. "The McDooleys."

"Are the McDooleys nice?" I ask as we dash over to the tree house.

"Yes," Lali says. "They're a married couple with twin girls who are a year older than me. They're eight."

"You're seven?" Jonah says happily, jogging along. "I'm seven!"

Lali smiles and gives another nod as she runs. "I'm the only seven-year-old in the whole kingdom. The McDooley twins are the closest to my age, but . . . they have each other." She says this last part a little sadly.

"I bet they'd love you if they got to know you," Jonah says.

"Maybe," Lali says. "I see them playing ball sometimes." She hesitates. "But I don't know if they would like me . . ."

"Of course they'd like you! Why would anyone not like you?" Jonah asks.

"Because . . . I don't know," she says. "I don't really have any friends."

I can't help but wonder if Lali believes all the mean things her grandmother says about her.

"We're your friends!" Jonah says.

"Don't you go to school?" I ask Lali.

She shakes her head. "There aren't enough kids here for a school. My mom teaches me when she's not working. And I read a lot."

Poor Little Red. She must be lonely.

We finally make it to the McDooleys' tree house. Up close it looks even bigger. This might be the biggest tree house I've ever seen — both inside and outside Howlton!

Lali leaps onto the ladder and starts propelling herself up with one hand.

"Awesome!" Jonah says, pumping his fist. He climbs up right behind her, holding Prince. Next is Nana and then me. I'm getting pretty good at climbing ladders, if I do say so myself.

Little Red reaches the landing and knocks on the tree house door. "Hello? Mr. and Mrs. McDooley? It's Little Red Riding Hood and some friends. May we come in? There's a wolf pack after us."

No answer.

She knocks again. "Hello?"

I peer in the window beside the door and gasp. "Is that a slide?" I ask.

I see a curving red slide that comes down from the ceiling.

Jonah hurries over and cups his eyes to block the glare from the sun. "And a ball pit? COOL!" He runs to the door and knocks. "Hello?" He knocks harder and the door swings open. I guess people in Howlton leave their doors unlocked since they figure wolves can't get in.

"The family might be away this weekend," Lali says. "The McDooley grandparents live a few towns over. In Hisss-ton."

"Hisss-ton?" I repeat.

"They have a lot of snakes," Lali explains.

Eep. Would that be worse than wolves?

"I wonder if the McDooleys would mind if we hide out in their tree house while they're gone," Nana says. "Just for a bit. Until the wolves are off our tail."

Ah-oooh! Ah-ooh!

Oh, no! The howling is getting closer.

Lali steps inside the house. "Whether they mind or not, it's an emergency!"

We all rush into the McDooleys' tree house. I close the door and turn around.

Wow.

chapter ten

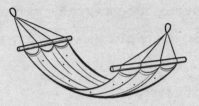

Tree House of Amusement

Oh. My. Goodness.

This is no ordinary tree house. It's more like a tree mansion. WITH AN AMUSEMENT PARK IN IT!

There's the huge red slide I saw before, plus the ball pit. There's also a tire swing, a trampoline, and lots of hammocks.

"This is incredible," I say.

"It really is," Lali says, looking around. "I've never been inside before! I know the McDooleys are wealthy. They manufacture most of the ladders in Howlton."

"Let's be respectful of their things," Nana warns us.

"Woo-hoo!" Jonah says, cannonballing into the ball pit. A bunch of red and blue balls go flying in the air. One lands on his head and then rolls off.

Prince leaps into the ball pit and disappears under the balls. Then he pops his head up. *Woof!* he says, jumping out and then jumping back in.

Nana laughs. "I have to admit, that does look like fun. Well, kids, if we have to hide out, this is the place to do it."

"Can I try the slide?" I ask Nana, pointing. The bright red slide curls around and around into the other side of the ball pit.

"Go ahead," Nana says. "Then we'll sit down and figure out how to save Owen."

Lali and I look at each other, and then we go racing up the ladder to the top of the slide. And who's right behind us? Nana!

Okay, occasionally she's annoying — like when she won't let me go to sleepovers — but come on, she's pretty amazing.

Lali slides down first. "Woo!" she calls as she goes round and round, her cape flowing behind her. She lands with a plunk underneath the balls. She's definitely loosened up since we met her.

Then it's my turn. "Whee!" I say, holding my arms up as I go careening down the slide. I land next to Lali and start laughing. "Awesome!" I say.

"Here comes Nana!" Nana says, and goes flying down the slide, landing under a heap of balls.

Her head pops up and she's grinning. "Let's definitely do that again."

After everyone takes a few more turns down the slide, we all bounce on the trampoline and swing on the tire swing. Then Lali, Nana, and I each take a hammock to rest in while Jonah and Prince explore the rest of the living room.

"This is my dream tree house for sure," Jonah says. "I wonder what this button does?" He points at a big silver button on what looks like a small frosted door carved inside the tree trunk.

Prince goes over and nudges the button with his nose.

"No, Prince!" I say. "It could be a trap or something!"

The little frosted door opens. Inside are bottles of drinks and cheese and fruit. There are also some wrapped packages marked HOT DOGS.

"It's a mini-fridge!" Lali exclaims.

"Wow," I say. "The McDooleys really know how to live."

"And they have ketchup in here," Jonah says. "Can we have something to eat?"

"That would be stealing," Nana says, frowning.

"We're already kind of breaking and entering," I say.

Nana shakes her head with a smile. "True. But that was necessary and eating their food isn't. Anyway, I brought some snacks." She reaches into her purse. "You should never leave the house without snacks. Or money! I have a twenty in my pocket."

"We never bring money or snacks into fairy tales," I admit.

"Well, you should," Nana says, handing out granola bars.

"The fairy tale kingdoms probably don't take American dollars," I say.

Nana laughs and winks at me. "Good point."

Lali, Jonah, and I all thank Nana as we unwrap the granola bars and start munching away.

"We need a plan," I say as I chew. "I know we're stuck here for now, but we have to save Owen before sunset."

I notice something hanging on the far wall. It's a map that says HOWLTON, and it shows the entire town: the path winding through the forest and the many tree houses of all different shapes, sizes, and colors. It's really clear. Like a Google Earth map.

I push myself out of the hammock and walk over to study the map. Lali and Jonah follow me.

"Here we are," I say, tapping the map. Which is easy because a little sign says: YOU ARE HERE. But seriously? You couldn't miss this tree mansion on the map.

"There's Dadi's tree cottage," Lali says, pointing to a spot not too far away from the tree mansion. "I recognize the flower boxes. And I live all the way over here." She points to the other edge of the map.

"And over there is the hunter's tree house," Jonah says, stepping closer to the map. "If you look closely, you can see the deer head through the window!"

We all examine the window. I can see the creepy dead amber eyes!

I shudder. And that hunter intends to hang Owen's head up on that wall.

I hear howling again from below. We can't leave to help Owen until the wolf pack is far enough away for us to go outside. Which means we're trapped — for now.

I look at my watch. "It's four thirty. We have about an hour and a half to save Owen. What do we do if we can't?"

Jonah raises his hand. Ooh! Maybe he has a good solution.

"I have to go to the bathroom," he says.

Or not.

"Let's go find it," Nana tells him. "I'm sure there are several in this tree mansion."

Nana and Jonah head out of the living room. Meanwhile, Lali and I get back into our hammocks while Prince plays with a stray ball from the ball pit.

Lali takes another bite of her granola bar. "Wow, your nana sure is nicer than my dadi," she says wistfully.

"Usually," I say. "Although I was invited to an amazing-sounding sleepover and she wouldn't let me go."

"Why not?" Lali asks.

"Because of 'family time,'" I say, making air quotes.

Lali tilts her head. "Family time? Like all of you spending time together?"

"Yup," I say, taking a bite of my own bar.

Lali looks confused. "Why would you want to leave when your nana is visiting? Don't you want to hang out with her? She seems so great."

"Well, she *is*," I say. "She makes us breakfast for dinner and reads us stories and plays games with us and watches fun movies with us."

Lali's eyes widen. "That sounds wonderful. I wish my dadi wanted to spend time with me. But she just wants me to bring her muffins and tea, and then she yells at me. She's always telling me to fix my bangs and to do a better job at ironing my cape."

"You're so nice to her, though," I say.

"Because it's important to me to treat her the way I want to be treated," Lali explains. "She and my mom are all I have. I'm lucky to have a family."

I know she's right. Of course she's right. I'm lucky to have my family, too. I'm lucky to have my nana. She always makes me feel wanted. And she always makes me feel like

I'm smart and brave and an amazing granddaughter. Even when I'm not acting like one.

"You're an amazing granddaughter," I tell Lali.

"Thanks," she says quietly.

"You really are," I say. "Even if your dadi doesn't tell you that you are, you are."

"Thanks," she says again, a little louder. She straightens her shoulders and looks pleased.

Nana and Jonah return to the living room.

I smile at Nana, and she smiles back.

"Guess what?" Jonah says. "The bathroom here is bigger than my bedroom at home!"

Suddenly, we hear howling below us again.

AH-OOH! AH-OOH!

Lali wrinkles her nose. "I hate when they all start howling together. It's extra creepy."

"It really is," I say.

The howling stops, and we can clearly hear the wolves talking outside.

"Where did they go?" Tina asks.

"They must have gone into the big tree house," one of the brothers says.

I shiver.

Then I climb out of my hammock and peek out the window. I see the three wolves standing below.

"We're just going to stay in here forever!" I yell out the window at them. "Sorry! You'll have to find your dinner somewhere else!" I stick my tongue out at them to emphasize my point. I need them to believe that we're not planning on going anywhere. I guess my plan is to fake them out.

"What are we going to do?" Lali whispers from her hammock. "We can't *really* stay here forever. My mom will get worried if I'm not home before dark. And we have to save Owen!"

I guess Jonah and I don't have to worry about getting home before morning, since the only person to worry about us — Nana — is right here. We just have to figure out *how* to get home. And get home before my parents do on Sunday!

Oh, no. Is Nana going to tell my parents about Maryrose and the mirror? If my parents find out, they might never let me and Jonah go into the mirror again! I shake the thought away. I'll have to beg Nana not to say anything later.

I watch as the wolves huddle together, discussing what to do. Finally, they all shrug and head down the path, disappearing from view. I wait for a while. Silence. I don't hear any more howling.

"Are the wolves gone?" Lali asks.

I look back out the window. I think they are. Did the plan work? I think it did! Woot! I am the world's best planner! I wonder if being a planner can be a job. Escape Planner, maybe?

Never mind, I still want to be a lawyer and then a judge.

I really do like the law.

I'll just pretend the whole breaking-and-entering-the-tree-mansion thing never happened.

"Come on," I call to the others. "The coast is clear. Now's our chance."

chapter eleven

Let's Make a Deal

"One last jump in the ball pit?" Nana asks.

"I like the way you think," Lali says.

"Just a quick one," I say.

"One, two, three," Jonah counts. "Cannonball!"

We all jump into the ball pit, Prince included. When we pop up for air, Jonah has a red ball stuck in his hair. Lali brushes it off, and Jonah blushes. Nana and I look at each other and grin. Jonah's crush on Lali is pretty cute.

"Okay, time to go," Nana says, pushing herself out of the pit first and then helping the rest of us out.

We straighten up the McDooleys' house the best we can, then head out the door.

We climb down the ladder, one by one, Lali leaping three rungs at a time. She really is good at climbing up and down ladders. Maybe she could be a professional ladder climber when she's older.

Is *that* a job? Probably not.

Once we're all on the ground, Jonah sets Prince down. We all look around. Still no sign of the wolf trio. Whew.

I glance at my watch. "And it's only five!"

"Perfect," Lali says. "We lost them! Let's head to the hunter's house."

We all start running along the path. I have no idea how Nana manages to run in those fuzzy slippers, but she does!

AH-OOOH HAHAHAHA!

NOOOOOOoooooo.

The really tall wolf steps into my path. His chest is white. He snarls and licks his lips. He's wearing a hat that says HARLEY on it.

"Oh, hello!" a female voice says. "Going somewhere?"

I whirl around. Staring right at me is Tina, her golden

eyes cold and mean. Her other brother, the short one whose fur is dark gray, is beside her, sharpening his claws against the tree trunk beside him. He must be Thurston.

They have us surrounded. Crumbs.

"Ha! Tricked you!" Tina says. "You thought we ran off, but we didn't! We knew you wouldn't stay in the tree house too long."

Yeah, I should probably forget about being an Escape Planner.

Harley bares his big, pointy teeth at us and lets out the loudest growl I've ever heard. I grab on to Nana's arm and Jonah grabs on to my arm. Lali grabs on to Jonah's arm, and Jonah blushes.

"Which one do you want for dinner, Tina?" the shorter wolf, Thurston, asks. His voice is surprisingly high for a wolf. It's almost birdlike. "I think I'll start with the mutt. He'll be my amuse-bouche." He licks his lips. He's looking right at Prince.

Prince growls back and then rushes behind Jonah's legs.

"Hmm, to be honest, none of them look all that appetizing," Tina says with a sneer.

Okay, that's good. We don't want to be appetizing to wolves.

"But I *am* really hungry," she says. "That dumb hunter is always on my trail, ready with that dumb bow and that dumb arrow whenever I'm about to nab a human."

Tina growls and snarls at me. How does a wolf get her teeth that sharp? Does she sharpen them with a nail file or something, or are they naturally like that? Her teeth are even bigger and sharper than Owen's.

"I think I'll have Little Red Riding Hood for lunch," Tina says, narrowing her golden eyes at Lali. "She's the one Owen has been trying to catch for months. His loss is my gain!"

Lali scowls, but I'm impressed that she doesn't look scared. "As if you could catch me. You might be fast, but I'm an expert climber and branch swinger!"

"Have you ever tried gymnastics?" Jonah asks Lali. "I bet you'd be really good at it."

Oh! She could be a gymnast! That is a much better job idea than professional ladder climber.

I should probably be focusing on the situation in front of me instead of worrying about what Little Red will be when she grows up.

Tina takes a step toward Lali. "We all know you're not

going anywhere," Tina says. "You'll never abandon your human pack to save yourself. You're too nice. I can tell."

"It's good to be nice!" Lali shouts.

"Good for *me*," Tina says with a laugh, baring her pointy teeth as she steps even closer to Little Red. "Although I really wish you'd take off that cape. I couldn't possibly digest that."

"Stop!" Jonah says, crossing his arms in front of his chest. "You can't eat Lali! We will not let you eat one of our pack!"

"Aww!" Lali says to him with a smile. "I'm part of your pack?"

"Of course," Jonah says, blushing again.

"Pack schmack!" Tina mutters. "You know who's part of *my* pack? My ridiculous brother Owen. And where is he? Off doing who knows what instead of being here with us."

"He can't be here with you," I say. "The hunter has him."

Tina's eyes narrow. "What?"

Oh! Tina clearly hates the hunter. I take a step toward her. Hmm. What's that phrase I once heard Mom say? *The enemy of your enemy is your friend.*

"We need your help!" I explain. "To save your brother. The hunter is going to kill Owen and hang his head on his trophy wall!"

"Ew," Tina says. "That's just creepy."

"Right?" I agree. Why didn't I ask the wolves for help sooner? Of course they'd help us — we're trying to save their brother. "So you'll come with us to save him?" I ask hopefully.

"Um . . . no," Tina snaps, her outrageously sharp white teeth glowing in the setting sun. "Survival of the fittest is the name of the game out here."

"What? Seriously?" I ask, shocked. "Come on. The hunter has Owen in his tree house *right* now. He's going to kill him at sunset and add him to his trophy-head wall! How could you not help? This is your brother we're talking about!"

"Who cares?" Tina asks, examining her claws, which I now notice are polished a sparkly light blue.

"Who cares? WHO CARES? Owen is your *family*," I say. "Family is everything!"

I dart a glance at Nana and Jonah and Prince. Family. My family.

"No, *meals* are everything," Tina says, advancing toward me. "Yummy food."

Argh. She's the worst. And all she cares about is food! What are we going to do?

Suddenly, I have an idea. "Oh, oh, oh! I know where you can get a really delicious, juicy hot dog. Do you like hot dogs?"

"I've never had a hot dog," she says. She points to Prince. "Will you just warm him up?"

Thurston and Harley look intrigued.

Prince stiffens, his ears flat against his head.

"Ew!" I scream. "No! You're not eating my dog! What's wrong with you? Hot dogs are not made of dog. They're made of . . . I don't know. But they are real food."

"And they're the best," Jonah chimes in. "Especially with ketchup."

"Or mustard," I add in case the three wolves like the same things as their brother.

Tina lifts her chin and studies me with her golden eyes. "Where can we get one?"

I turn to Nana. "I know you said it was stealing, but this is urgent!" I whisper.

"It is urgent," Nana says, nodding. "Plus, I will leave the McDooleys my twenty dollars and a note. That seems fair, considering the circumstances. I know it's American dollars, but . . ."

"It's the thought that counts?" Jonah asks.

"In this case, yes," Nana says.

I turn back to the wolves. "When we were hiding in the tree house, we saw some delicious-looking hot dogs in the fridge. What if we give you those? Then you can have your dinner and we can go save your brother."

Tina rolls her eyes. "Honestly, why bother? But I guess we owe him *something*."

"Frankly," Nana tells the wolves, hands on her hips, "I think you should be ashamed of yourselves." She stares down Tina, Thurston, and Harley. "Your brother needs you, and all you care about are your stomachs!"

"That's right," Tina says. "Now, get me those hot dogs, and you're free to go."

"Fine!" I snap.

The five of us turn and start to walk back toward the McDooleys' tree mansion.

"Oh, no, you don't!" Tina snarls, grabbing Nana's arm.

I gasp, but Nana remains calm. "The old lady is staying with us. Collateral. If you don't come back with the food, she's dinner."

"Her name is *Nana*!" I mutter. "Show some respect!"

"Whatever," Tina says, licking her lips. "Now, get me my dinner!"

"They can't take Nana!" Jonah cries, reaching for her. I pull him away. I don't want to leave Nana behind with the wolves, either, but we have no other choice.

"I'll be fine," Nana insists, nodding at us. "But hurry back."

chapter twelve

A Trade

I hate leaving Nana with that horrible pack of hungry wolves. But what can I do? As long as I come back with the food, Nana will be fine. And then we can go save Owen.

Jonah, Lali, Prince, and I go climbing back up the ladder to the tree mansion. Lali catapults herself up to the middle of the ladder, taking the rungs by threes. Jonah's up in two seconds with Prince under his arm. Then I hurry up the rungs as fast as I can.

While I catch my breath, Jonah and Lali rush inside. Jonah heads right for the mini-fridge on the tree trunk.

"Press the button!" I say.

He does.

Nothing happens.

"Press harder!" Lali orders.

He does. Still nothing!

"Let me try," I say, running over. I press the button in as hard as I can. *Please open*, I beg the frosted door. *Pleeeease!*

It still doesn't open.

Ahhh! We can't return without the hot dogs! Or Nana will be dinner!

I press again. The door doesn't budge. No, no, no. There is no time for this!

Jonah peers more closely at the button. "It's stuck on the side," he says. "See that edge is a little bent in?"

Nooo! "We have to get that fridge open," I say. "It's the only way to save Nana!"

"Stand back, people," Lali says.

We do. She steps back, too, and takes a running leap, her leg outstretched toward the button. Her foot hits the button really hard and the door pops open.

"Yeah!" Jonah shouts. "Go, Lali!"

Lali beams.

"You should really start a gymnastics team," I tell her.

"I don't know what that is, but it sounds fun!" she says. She grabs the hot dogs and buns. "Do we have to cook them?" she asks.

"Hot dogs are pre-cooked. And anyway, the wolves eat people," Jonah says. "And they were about to eat Prince. I think they'll be okay with cold meat."

"Good point," I say.

"But I'll give them some ketchup," Jonah says, grabbing a ketchup bottle and squirting some onto each hot dog. "Just to help the taste."

I grab pretzels, too, plus some cake — confetti cake! — and some of the drinks. I leave the McDooleys a quick note to explain, plus Nana's twenty dollars, on the kitchen counter. Lali grabs a shopping bag from a closet, puts the food inside, and then we all rush out.

We scamper down the ladder and run as fast as we can back to where the wolf pack is holding Nana hostage for the food. I can see Nana backed up against a tree, the wolves guarding her.

"Yay!" Nana says. "Here come the kids!"

Tina turns around. "Took you long enough, slowpokes."

"Are you okay, Nana?" I ask worriedly. "They didn't hurt you?"

"I'm absolutely fine," Nana says. "I knew I could count on you."

I smile and give her a hug.

"Keep the annoying family chitchat for later," Tina snaps, snatching the shopping bag out of Lali's hands. "Let me make sure everything is here." She pokes her snout in, then looks back at us. "Fine. Go. Save my useless brother."

Nana gives Tina an angry stare. "I'm very disappointed in you."

"Whatevs!" Tina says, handing her brothers a hot dog each. "Oooh, is that confetti cake?" she adds, licking her lips.

With the wolf pack busy stuffing their faces, we rush away toward the tree house.

My watch says that it's five forty-five. I see that the sun is about to drop into the horizon. Which means we're running out of time. Owen's running out of time.

"Owen, we're coming!" I shout.

We arrive at the hunter's tree house. The hunter's horse is tied to a tree, and he looks sad. Lali scratches him behind the ears, and he whinnies. Aw.

Then we make a plan. Lali and Jonah decide to climb up a tree across from the hunter's house to try to see inside. Meanwhile, Nana, Prince, and I hide behind another tree, waiting for them to come back with the scoop.

Soon, Jonah and Lali rush back over to us.

"I saw Owen! He's waking up!" Lali says. "He's on the floor and rubbing his head. And the hunter is sitting at his desk, sharpening his arrows!"

That does not sound good. Nothing good comes from sharpening arrows.

"I'm going to reason with the hunter," Nana says. "Wish me luck."

She strides toward his tree house and starts climbing up the ladder.

"Good luck, Nana!" I call out nervously. I run to a closer tree so I can see what's happening. Lali, Jonah, and Prince follow me.

Nana reaches the tree house door and knocks. "Hello! Huntsman! Open up! I need to talk to you!"

I watch as the door opens and the hunter appears. His beard looks even scruffier than it did before, even though it's only been a few hours. When he sees Nana, he scowls. "It's you!" he yells.

Nana looks surprised. "Yes. Have we met?"

"Not officially," he snaps. "But I watched you run away from my tree house after you knocked me unconscious!"

Uh-oh.

"What in the world are you talking about?" Nana asks, clearly confused.

"I was in the bathroom, and I heard someone moving around in my house," the huntsman explains angrily. "I came out to see a young girl looking at my animal heads, and then someone else attacked me from behind!" The hunter frowns at Nana. "When I came to, I spotted *you* leaving my tree house! Which means — you attacked me!"

"I did not!" Nana says, aghast.

"If it wasn't you, then who else could it have been?"

Jonah and I exchange a glance.

"Oops," Jonah mutters. "Um, Mr. Hunter . . ." He steps out from behind the tree.

"Jonah, shush!" Nana says, waving her hand down at us, behind her back. "I'm sorry. It was an accident, though. I apologize."

"*She* apologizes?" Jonah says.

Nana is taking the blame for Jonah!

"Apology not accepted," the hunter says. "Now, go away. I have a wolf to attend to."

"But —" Nana reaches out to stop him. As she does, I see her slipper slide on the top rung of the ladder.

And the next thing I know, Nana is falling to the ground.

chapter thirteen

A Pet Wolf

noooo! Nana's fall must be happening super fast, but to me it looks like it's in slow motion. We have to catch her! But how?

Lali leaps toward the ladder, whips off her cape, holds on to one side, and screams at me and Jonah: "Hold this!"

Oh. Yes!

Jonah and I each grab a side of the cape just as Nana lands —

WHOMP!

Nana lands right in the middle of the cape.

Her weight brings all three of us down, but the cape definitely broke her fall.

WHEW.

"Nana, are you okay?" I ask from the ground.

"I . . . think so . . ." Nana says, trembling as she brushes herself off and climbs to her feet. "Well, that was frightening! And also a little exciting." She catches her breath. "Thank you, everyone! That was quick thinking, Lali."

"You're welcome," Lali says, smiling. "The cape is really strong, what can I say?"

"It wasn't the cape that saved Nana," Jonah tells Lali. "It was you."

"Can you all go home now?" the hunter calls down from his doorway. "You're ruining my good mood."

What a jerk.

"I saw Owen behind the hunter," Nana says. "He's awake and scared."

We saved Nana, but we still haven't saved Owen. What should we do?

Clomp-clomp. Clomp-clomp!

The hunter narrows his eyes at us, then looks farther down the path toward the clomp-clomp sound.

Is that a horse galloping? Yes! And it's coming our way!

I stare at the path as the galloping sound gets closer.

Finally, around a curve comes a black horse with two people sitting on it. Up front is a woman with a long brown braid streaked with gray, wearing a short green dress and a matching green cowgirl hat. And riding behind her is . . . Dadi! In her yellow lace bathrobe, sleeping cap, and glasses!

They come to a stop in front of the hunter's tree house.

"The huntsman's house again?" the woman on the horse says to Dadi. "I was sent here before, but nobody was home."

"Hi, Mona," Lali says.

Oh! Mona! Policewoman, firewoman, AND doctor!

Mona gets off the horse and helps Dadi down. She hands Dadi the white cane that I noticed in the tree cottage earlier.

"That's him, Officer!" Dadi tells Mona, pointing up at the hunter. "Arrest him at once!"

"Dadi? What are you doing here?" Lali asks.

"I thought you guys might need some help," Dadi says. "I called Mona and told her there was an emergency. She came to get me immediately."

"She scared me," Mona admits. Then she glares up at the tree house. "But you! Huntsman! You need to hand over the wolf immediately."

"I do not!" the huntsman says. "There is no law against hunting animals in Howlton."

"No law at all?" I ask. This town needs some new lawyers.

"No," Mona says. "There are no hunting laws about wild animals."

Wait. "What about *non*-wild animals?" I ask, an idea forming in my mind.

"You mean domesticated animals?" Mona asks. "Well, yes. Hunting a domesticated animal is illegal."

"Then . . ." I say, thinking fast. "It's a good thing that Owen is Dadi's pet! He's a domesticated animal!"

Everyone freezes.

"That's ridiculous," the hunter says. "This wolf is not Dadi's domesticated animal. She can't prove that."

Dadi clears her voice. "Yes, I can. He's wearing my pearl necklace. Aren't you, Owen?"

Yes, yes, yes! Way to go, Dadi!

"Come show us!" Mona hollers.

Owen appears at the doorway beside the hunter, looking woozy. He is indeed still wearing Dadi's pearl necklace.

"You're coming with me!" Mona tells the hunter, climbing up the ladder.

"No way," the hunter says. He stretches his arrow straight at her.

Noooo!

"Oh, no, you don't!" Dadi shouts.

Then she throws her cane up, up, up at the door. And somehow it hits the hunter square in the head. He falls backward into his house. *Plunk.*

"His poor head is getting a lot of damage today," I say.

"Great aim, Dadi," Lali says.

"I used to play basketball," she says.

"You did?" Lali asks. "I didn't know that!"

"You don't know everything about me," Dadi says, straightening her shoulders. "I wasn't always such a helpless old lady."

"You're not a helpless old lady," Lali says quickly. "You never have been and you never will be."

"Well . . . thanks," Dadi says.

I glance up at Nana and squeeze her hand. I have a whole new appreciation for grandmas.

"You're under arrest, Huntsman!" Mona says, climbing

up the ladder. "For attempted murder of a domesticated animal and for trying to shoot me with an arrow." She throws the unconscious huntsman over her shoulder and climbs down the ladder. Then she gets back on her horse. "See you guys later. I'm going to drop Huntsman off at the prison. Then I have some house calls to make. It's allergy season."

We wave good-bye and Mona goes trotting off. The huntsman's horse, still tied to the tree, whinnies happily. He must not have liked the huntsman very much, either.

"Yay!" I say. "Dadi saved the day."

"You did, Dadi! Thank you!" Lali exclaims.

"Less talk, more getting me my cane," Dadi snaps.

"Dadi, please," Lali says. "Do you have to be SO grumpy all the time?"

Oh, wow. Nana, Jonah, and I all look at one another. Did Lali really just say that? It's the first time she's talked back to her grandmother!

"I . . ." Dadi's face turns bright red. "I'm not THAT grumpy!"

"Yes, you are," Lali says, her voice firm. "And when you criticize me constantly, it hurts my feelings. I feel like

I can't do anything right! It makes me feel like I'm not a good granddaughter." She glances down at her red sneakers.

"Oh, my dear Lali. You're a superb granddaughter," Dadi says sadly. "I am so sorry I made you feel anything less than that. I *can* be a real grump, can't I?" She sighs. "I guess I'm just lonely since your grandfather died. And it's tough to have to depend so much on those around you. It really does make a person feel helpless."

"So why don't you move in with me and my mom?" Lali asks.

"Because then I'm *really* depending on you! And I love my tree house! It reminds me of your grandfather. I don't want to move. You can't make me!"

Lali sighs. "I won't. I love you, Dadi."

Dadi's eyes tear up. "You're so good to me, Lali. I love you, too."

Awww!

"How sweet!" says an icy voice behind us. "So sweet I might vomit!"

I recognize that voice.

Tina.

Crumbs.

I turn around. She, Thurston, and Harley are all back. Teeth bared.

"We're still hungry," Tina says. "Those hot dogs were good, but not filling enough. And why are they called hot dogs when they're cold? Anyway, Lali and Dadi, you're mine. Thurston, you take the boy and the mutt. Harley, you can have the old lady and the girl."

Nooo!

The wolf pack has us surrounded. Even though there are more of us than them — Owen doesn't count because he's still up in the tree house. Plus, he's still wobbly from the effects of the sleeping medicine.

That makes five humans and one small dog — oh, and the huntsman's horse — against three wolves. But the ones with the claws and super-sharp teeth have the advantage.

I crane my neck to see if Mona is still in shouting distance, but I don't even hear the clomps of her horse's hooves anymore.

We're on our own.

"We made a deal!" I remind Tina. "We gave you the hot dogs to leave us alone. We even threw in drinks! And confetti cake!"

Tina smirks. "No, you gave us the food so we'd let you save Owen. And you did. So now you're our dessert. Our second dessert." She laughs as though that's hilarious.

"No fair!" Jonah says. "You tricked us!"

"So sue us," Harley says, brushing a fallen dead leaf off his leather jacket.

"Yeah!" Thurston adds, puffing out his chest to make himself seem taller. "We're wolves, not people. We don't make deals."

Owen appears in the doorway of the tree house again. He still looks kind of groggy. "Hey! Stop it right now," he warns his siblings. "These people saved my life! Doesn't that mean anything to you? They're my friends."

"Stop your whining!" Tina says, staring up at him. "I'm hungry, and that's it. They're our dessert."

"No! Leave my friends alone!" Owen insists. He slowly climbs down the ladder and lands in front of his sister. He lets out a mighty growl. "When you feel strongly about something," Owen says to his siblings, "you have to stick up for what you believe. And these people are my friends. They saved my life. Now I'm saving theirs."

"But, Owey!" Thurston whines. "I'm hungry!"

"Shut it," Tina snaps. "Owen's made his decision. He chose *them* over us."

Owen rolls his eyes and turns toward Thurston. "I just don't like eating humans, okay? There are a lot of other things to eat!"

"Like hot dogs," says Harley. "They *were* really tasty. What's in hot dogs, if not actual dogs, anyway?"

"No one knows for sure," I say.

"They're a mystery," Jonah adds. "Better not to know."

"I hope you don't think you're coming home with us," Tina says to Owen.

"Listen here, young lady," Nana says, wagging a finger at Tina. "Owen may be a different kind of wolf, but he's still your brother. And don't you forget it!"

Tina growls at Nana.

"You're *family*," I tell Tina. "That's what Nana is saying."

"I don't want to go with them," Owen says. "Why would I go with someone who was going to let me get hurt?"

"Suit yourself," Tina says. "We'll leave you and your little friends alone, but you better find somewhere else to live. We're done with you."

"Let's go look for more hot dogs," Harley says.

"We should call them hot *wolves*," Thurston suggests as the three of them run off.

Owen sighs. "I guess that's that," he says with a sad expression. Poor guy.

"I'm sorry your family doesn't realize how special you are," Nana says to him.

"Thank you," he replies softly. "I'm sorry, too."

"Maybe they'll come around one day," Dadi says. She puts her arm around Lali. "Some of us do."

"Maybe," Owen says.

"Thank you for standing up for us," Lali says to Owen. "You saved us."

"You're welcome," he says. "It was the right thing to do. And it was only fair. You saved me."

I glance at my watch and then I nod at Jonah.

"We should probably get going," I tell my brother. "Owen is safe and so are Nana and Lali. So our job here is done. And it's almost morning. That's when we normally go through the mirror," I explain to Nana.

Nana puts her arm around me. "Is it almost morning already?" She yawns. "You know, Abby, maybe you *could* go to your friend Penny's house for breakfast after all."

My heart expands. "Really? You don't mind?"

She smiles. "No. I don't. We got to spend so much extra time together on this adventure! When we get home, I can drive you over to Penny's if you still want to go."

"I do want to go! I do! Thank you!" I give Nana a tight hug. "You're amazing."

"*You're* amazing. I'm so proud of you. Both of you," she says, pulling Jonah in for a group hug.

"Now we just have to figure out what the portal is," I say. "Hmm. Could it be inside the hunter's house?"

"I'll check it out," Jonah offers.

"I'll come with you," Lali says.

"Wait until you see all the creepy animal heads!" Jonah tells Lali. "Are you coming, Abby?"

"I think I'll stay here," I say. "Seeing them once was enough."

In a little while, Jonah and Lali come back down.

"We knocked on everything," Jonah says. "Nothing swirled."

"You know, Owen," Lali says thoughtfully, "if we took

the creepy heads off the walls and put up some band posters, you could live in the hunter's house while he's in jail."

"Thanks," Owen says. "But living all by myself? Sounds kind of lonely. Wolves are pack animals, you know? But don't worry about me. Let's just figure out how to get you guys home. Where else could the portal be?"

"Could it be at Dadi's house?" Jonah suggests.

"I can't walk all the way back there!" Dadi grumbles. "Even with my cane."

"Well, luckily there's a horse right here," Lali says, untying the huntsman's horse. He whinnies gratefully and Lali rubs his ears. She really is good with animals.

So Dadi and Nana end up riding back to Dadi's tree cottage on the huntsman's horse, while Lali, Jonah, Prince, Owen, and I walk alongside them.

When we get back to the tree cottage, the huntsman's horse nibbles on some grass. Meanwhile, we all climb up the ladder. It takes Dadi a full five minutes to make her way up, but she does with our help.

"That was a lot of activity," she says once we're inside. "I need a rest, I think."

Nana and Lali help Dadi settle into bed. Lali pulls the quilt over her.

"Wait, Dadi," Lali says. "Before you take a nap, I have an idea."

"Yes?" Dadi asks.

Lali glances from her grandmother to Owen. "Now you know you won't have to be afraid of Owen. He's kind and friendly. And I'm wondering if you would let him stay with you in the tree cottage. You can be companions! And in exchange for letting him live here, he can protect you from the other wolves."

Owen grins at Dadi. "I would love that. I need a pack. You could be my new pack!"

I can't help but grin, too.

"Doesn't everyone think that's a good idea?" Lali asks, looking at all of us.

"Yes!" I say.

"Pack it up!" Nana says.

"Pack it in!" Jonah says.

Woof! Prince adds.

"Let me have a good look at you, wolf," Dadi says, adjusting her round eyeglasses.

Owen takes a step toward the bed.

"Well, come closer!" Dadi barks. "I don't bite! Even with my teeth in!"

Dadi gives Owen the once-over. "Hmm. You ARE quite majestic-looking. And I do like your yellow-gold eyes. But if you intend to bunk here, you'll have to let me brush your fur every morning," she insists. "I mean, look at that matted coat. Sit down by me this instant."

Owen tiptoes closer to the bed, looking a little nervous. He sits down next to Dadi.

Dadi picks up the brush on the table. She begins brushing his fur.

"Tee-hee!" Owen says, laughing. "That tickles!"

"Stop moving so much!" Dadi admonishes, continuing to brush him. She puts the brush down and looks him over. "There, good as new."

Owen does look well-groomed now.

"Can you cook?" she asks.

"Me?"

"Yes, you! I have grocery money. So if I give it to you with a shopping list and then some recipes, can you buy us food and make it?"

Owen nods. "I'd love to cook," he says. "I bet I'd make great roasted potatoes, if Nana could give me her recipe. I'm a quick learner."

"I'd be happy to," Nana says, taking a pen and paper out of her purse.

"I can teach you to bake, too," Lali says. "Plus, it seems we have a new horse." She nods out the window. "I'm sure Mona will let you borrow him for now, if you take care of him. And Dadi can get around more easily on a horse."

"Perfect," Dadi says. "But, Owen? There's something you better know —"

"Yes?"

"You can't keep my pearls. I'm saving them for Lali." Dadi smiles at her granddaughter. Owen shrugs and removes the pearl necklace, handing it back to Dadi.

Lali beams. "Thank you, Dadi. So does this mean that Owen can live here with you?" she asks hopefully.

Dadi smiles. "He can."

"Yay!" I exclaim.

Owen gives Dadi a lick on the arm. She laughs and pats his big, furry back.

"So you'll be my family?" Owen asks.

Dadi nods.

Aw.

"Hey, guess what?" Jonah whispers.

"What?" I say.

"Wolves DO wag their tails."

I laugh, watching Owen's big, furry tail moving from side to side with obvious joy.

Hurrah. I glance at Jonah and Nana. I'm lucky to have been born into such an amazing family — and Owen is lucky to have made his own.

"Abby," Nana says, "if you want to get to that breakfast, we should keep looking for the portal."

Right! The portal.

While Dadi and Owen chat about recipes, Jonah, Lali, Nana, and I start looking around the house. We knock on the bed. On the wall. On the door. On the fireplace. Nothing swirls. Nothing turns purple. No portals here, either. Hmm.

"If we do find it," Jonah says, "can Lali come home with us?" He sheepishly darts a glance at her. "She could go to school with me. She'd love school! And we have a gymnastics team."

Lali smiles. "That sounds fun, but I can't leave my dadi or my mom. I love them. And they love me."

"I do," Dadi says. "I really do. And even though Owen is here, I still expect you to visit every day, young lady."

"I will," Lali promises. "Plus, I was also thinking of calling the McDooley twins. Maybe they'd want to play with me sometime."

"They'd be lucky to have you as a friend," Jonah says.

Owen clears his throat. "Will you still bring your basket of goodies when you come?" he asks Lali. "It would be great if you did. I really enjoyed your muffins."

"Of course!" she says.

"The *basket*!" I exclaim. "Maybe that's the portal."

"Terrific idea," Nana says. "Where is it?"

Lali gets the basket from the kitchen and hands it to me.

I hold the basket in one hand and knock on it with the other. Suddenly, the whole basket starts to shake. It *is* the portal!

"Hurrah!" Nana says. "Abby, you are really good at this fairy tale thing."

I feel myself glow. "Thank you."

"I'm really so impressed with you both," Nana says to

me and Jonah. "You guys are much braver than I was at your age."

"Well," I say, ruffling Jonah's hair. "It helps that I have a sidekick."

"You didn't even want me to come with you today," Jonah reminds me, raising an eyebrow.

"That would have been a big mistake," I tell him.

"A HUGE mistake," he says.

"Massive." I grin and squeeze his shoulder.

"I guess it's time to say good-bye," Nana says.

"Already?" Jonah says, looking at Lali with a frown.

"Already," Nana says. "Good-bye, Dadi. Good-bye, Owen. Good-bye, Lali. It was a pleasure to meet you."

She gives everyone a quick hug, and I do the same.

"Bye, everyone," Jonah says. He blushes. "Good-bye, Lali."

"Good-bye, Jonah," Lali says. And then she leans over and gives him a quick kiss on the cheek.

Jonah turns the color of her cape. "I'll miss you," he says. "I hope I get to see you again, one day."

So sweet. I hope he gets to see her again one day, too.

The inside of the basket is purple and swirling. We have to jump in now!

But it's so small.

"How do we fit?" I wonder.

"I have an idea," Nana says. "Something I tried years ago when I was in a similar situation. It worked then, so maybe . . ."

"What is it?" I ask.

Nana holds the basket with her right hand and puts her left one inside. "Abby, Jonah, and Prince, put one hand — and paw — in the basket, on top of mine."

We do as she says.

Suddenly, I feel my feet rise off the ground. The basket is swirling, but so are we! It's working!

It's like we're on a Tilt-A-Whirl.

The basket is getting bigger now and sucking us inside!

"Bye, everyone!" I call to Lali, Dadi, and Owen.

"Bye!" they call back.

Ah-ooh! Owen howls as we leave them.

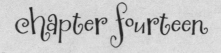

chapter fourteen

Dinner for Breakfast

a moment later, I land on the familiar floor of our basement in Smithville.

Nana's technique worked! Yes! How incredible is
my nana?

I check to make sure we'll all here. Yup, we are! There's
Jonah, jumping up from the basement floor and brushing off
his pajamas. And Prince, running in excited circles. And there's
Nana, looking at the magic mirror bolted onto the wall.

Aww, she's staring at the mirror so longingly. She must
miss going into stories. I sure am glad Nana went into *Little
Red Riding Hood* with us.

"I can't believe you had a portal when you were a kid, Nana," I say.

Nana turns from the mirror to me and smiles. "You and Jonah are very lucky," she says. "You've had amazing adventures. With more to come."

The mirror begins swirling in the center. Yay! That means Maryrose, the fairy who lives in our mirror, is going to talk to us.

The outline of Maryrose's face and her long wavy hair appear in the mirror.

"Hello, Nana!" Maryrose says. "I'm glad you got to join your grandchildren in the story."

Nana grins. "It was wonderful going into a fairy tale. Just like when I was a girl. Except this time, I didn't just watch. I helped out."

"You more than helped out," I say to Nana. "I don't know what I would have done without you."

"Me neither!" Jonah says. We both wrap Nana in a hug.

"Do you remember what we discussed?" Maryrose asks Nana gently. "How I must remain a secret?"

Nana nods. "Yes, I understand the rules." She looks at me and Jonah. "I won't tell your parents about this. I don't

151

like keeping secrets from them, but I know this is a special case."

WHEW. "Thank you, Nana," I say, feeling even more grateful.

Nana nods. "Well, it's important that you keep trying to free Maryrose from the mirror," she says.

"I have faith in them," Maryrose says. "And Abby and Jonah, now you know why you were chosen to go into stories."

I do?

Wait a minute! I do!

"Because going into stories runs in our family!" I say. It just skipped a generation.

Oooooh. Now it all makes sense! I knew it couldn't be a coincidence that our nana had a magic portal and we do, too.

"Exactly," Maryrose says. "I knew you were the right ones. And your nana has prepared you well."

"She really has," I say, thinking of *The Big Book of Fairy Tales*. "And one day, Maryrose," I promise, "we will get you out of that mirror!"

Maryrose smiles and then the mirror starts rippling.

That always means Maryrose is going back deeper inside the mirror. After a minute, she's gone.

"Well," Nana says, "I guess it's time for Abby to go to Penny's. Why don't you call her and let her know you're coming?"

I nod, but I don't find myself rushing for the phone.

We all head up the stairs. Prince stops on the main level to curl up in his dog bed in the kitchen. Nana, Jonah, and I go up to the second floor. Then Jonah goes into his room, and I go into mine.

"Wait. Nana!" I say. "Come look at the jewelry box you gave me. Every time I come back from a story, the characters change to show what happened."

Nana and I turn the jewelry box around until we see Lali. She's wearing her red hood and hanging upside down from high beams in the ceiling of Dadi's tree cottage. Two identical twin girls are hanging beside her. They must be the McDooley twins. Yay! Lali has friends now. And they are doing gymnastics!

And Dadi and the wolf are sitting on the bed, playing cards and smiling.

"Wow," Nana says, looking at all the different characters on the jewelry box. "You've done some amazing things, Abby. I'm so proud of you." She hands me her phone. "Here you go. Call Penny. I'll get the car keys."

I stare at the phone. "Um, Nana?" I say. "I don't need to go to Penny's. I'll see her at school on Monday. You're only here for two days."

"Are you sure?" Nana asks.

I nod. "Completely sure. I'm so lucky to have you. You love me even when I'm acting like a spoiled brat."

She pulls me into a hug. "You're never a spoiled brat!"

"A rude brat, then," I say, inhaling her Nana-ness.

She laughs. "Abby, I understand that you want to spend time with your friends. I just miss you."

"And I miss you. And I'm sorry if I was rude before. Really sorry. I love you."

"I love you, too," Nana says.

"For the record, *I* never acted like a rude or a spoiled brat!" Jonah calls out, sticking his head into my room.

Nana and I laugh.

"Who's hungry?" Nana asks.

"Me!" Jonah and I both say.

"Can we have dinner for breakfast?" Jonah asks.

"How about tuna melts on the bagels I got?" Nana asks, leading us downstairs to the kitchen.

"Mmm," I say. Perfect.

"Can you tell us stories while we eat?" Jonah asks Nana when we reach the kitchen.

"What kind of stories?" Nana asks.

"About your adventures in the fairy tales!" he says. "Especially *Jack and the Beanstalk*!"

"Yes, please!" I say.

"Absolutely," Nana says, taking the orange juice out of the fridge. "And I want to hear about all of *your* adventures."

"We'll tell you everything," Jonah says.

"Yes," I say. "Everything. All of our fairy tale secrets."

Jonah and I sit down together at the kitchen table while Nana makes the tuna melts.

"I love my human pack," Jonah says, looking around with a smile.

"Me too," I say.

Woof! Prince adds, trotting over to the table. And he wags his tail just like Owen did.

acknowledgments

A hundred thank-you muffins and hot thermoses of tea to:

Everyone at Scholastic: Aimee Friedman (so many muffins!), Rachel Feld, Vaishali Nayak, Mindy Stockfield, Monica Palenzuela, Charisse Meloto, Lauren Donovan, Tracy van Straaten, Robin Hoffman, Melissa Schirmer, Elizabeth Parisi, Abby McAden, David Levithan, Lizette Serrano, Emily Heddleson, Sue Flynn, Olivia Valcarce, and everyone in the School Channels and Sales.

My amazing agents, Laura Dail and Tamar Rydzinski, and queen of publicity, Deb Shapiro.

Lauren Walters, Alyssa Stonoha, Mitali Dave, Katie Rose Summerfield, who do all the stuff.

Thank you to all my friends, family, writing buddies, and first readers: Targia Alphonse, Tara Altebrando, Bonnie Altro, Elissa Ambrose, Robert Ambrose, Jennifer Barnes, Emily Bender, the Bilermans, Jess Braun, Jeremy Cammy, Avery Carmichael, the Dalven-Swidlers, Julia DeVillers, Elizabeth Eulberg, the Finkelstein-Mitchells,

Stuart Gibbs, Alan Gratz, Adele Griffin, Anne Heltzel, Emily Jenkins, Lauren Kisilevsky, Maggie Marr, Aviva Mlynowski, Larry Mlynowski, Lauren Myracle, Melissa Senate, Courtney Sheinmel, Jennifer E. Smith, Christina Soontornvat, the Swidlers, Robin Wasserman, Louisa Weiss, Rachel and Terry Winter, the Wolfes, Maryrose Wood, and Sara Zarr.

Extra love and thanks to my pack: Chloe, Anabelle, and Todd.

And to my Whatever After readers: Thank you for reading my books! I heart you. Call your nanas.

THUD.

We land on a patch of hay in what seems to be a small barn. Its walls are made of weathered wood. And it definitely smells like a barn — like when you visit a petting zoo. I don't see any animals, though.

Is there a barn in *Jack and the Beanstalk*?

Please let there be a barn in *Jack and the Beanstalk*.

Prince gets up and starts sniffing the one corral, which is empty. Jonah stands up and stretches and pulls hay off his pj's. He sighs loudly. He's clearly not cheered up yet.

Through the small window, light spills into the barn. I stand up to look outside. It's daytime, but overcast and foggy.

"I bet you don't see a beanstalk," Jonah says grumpily.

"Um . . . I don't," I admit. All I can see is a very small house. It's made of the same weathered brown wood as the barn and has a brick chimney on the roof. The house and barn are surrounded by a rickety brown fence and, beyond that, rolling green hills. "But we're somewhere in the country. Beanstalks grow in the country!" I add hopefully.

Prince barks, as if he agrees.

Jonah groans. "Forget it. We're definitely not in *Jack and the Beanstalk*. Maybe Maryrose can let us go back now — "

Moo! Mooo!

I freeze. A cow! I just heard a cow moo from somewhere outside! At least I think it was a cow. Nothing else makes a moo sound.

There is definitely a cow in *Jack and the Beanstalk*. It's one of the most important parts of the story!

"Did you hear that, Jonah?" I ask excitedly. "Did you? It's a cow! It mooed!"

"So what?" Jonah says, but there's a teeny bit of interest in his voice.

I move around to the other end of the window, and I see something! Yes!

A skinny woman about my mom's age is sitting on a stool in front of a super-skinny brown cow. The woman is wearing a tattered gray dress and threadbare brown shoes. A yellow bandana is tied around her head and she's holding a tin pail under the cow.

"Come on, Princess Milka," the woman says to the cow. "Be a love and give us some milk, will ya?"

My eyes widen. "Jonah, come see!" I hiss, and he hurries over to join me by the window.

We watch the woman squeeze the cow's udders like I've seen farmers do at the state fair. I, personally, have never milked a cow. And I am not sure I ever want to.

"Is the cow named Princess Milka in *Jack and the Beanstalk*?" Jonah whispers.

I try to remember the story from when our nana read it to us. "Princess Milka doesn't sound familiar. But I don't know. There are a few versions of *Jack and the Beanstalk*," I say. I know the basic story, but I haven't read it in a while. Don't tell Jonah.

Moo, the cow says again. *Moooooooooo.*

The woman sighs. "Not a drop of milk out of ya — for the seventh day in a row!" she groans. "Your milk was all we had to sell at the market for money. Now what'll we do? We have no money and very little food left. I'll have to sell you."

"She'll have to sell her!" I say to Jonah. "Did you hear that? That is exactly what happens in *Jack and the Beanstalk*. Exactly! Jack's mom wants to sell the cow. That must be

Jack's mom." I grab my brother's arm. "Jonah, we're in the story! We have to be!"

Jonah's eyes are the size of saucers. "Are you sure?"

I don't want to promise anything yet, but it seems VERY likely.

Then we both hear the woman say, "I'll ask Jack to take you to the market, Princess Milka."

JACK?

She said Jack!

Jonah and I gasp at the same time, and glance at each other. We did it! We're in *Jack and the Beanstalk*. For real! Wahoo!

"I can't believe it," Jonah whispers. "We're really here."

"Come on," I say happily. "Let's go introduce ourselves. We can ask to meet Jack!"

I open the door to the barn and step outside. The weather is weird. It's neither warm nor cold and there's a mist in the air — not quite a drizzle like you'd need a raincoat, but my curly hair is probably getting even curlier from all the humidity.

I expect Jonah to run over to the woman. To hurl

himself at her. To fly. This is it. We're going to meet Jack.

But Jonah freezes in the doorway. He takes a step back. And another step.

"No," he says.

Huh?

"I don't . . . I don't want to meet Jack," he says. With a jolt, he turns around and disappears into the barn.

Read all the Whatever After books!

Whatever After #1. FAIREST of ALL

In their first adventure, Abby and Jonah wind up in the story of Snow White. But when they stop Snow from eating the poisoned apple, they realize they've messed up the whole story! Can they fix it — and still find Snow her happy ending?

Whatever After #2: IF the SHOE FITS

This time, Abby and Jonah find themselves in Cinderella's story. When Cinderella breaks her foot, the glass slipper won't fit! With a little bit of magic, quick thinking, and luck, can Abby and her brother save the day?

Whatever After #3: SINK or SWIM

Abby and Jonah are pulled into the tale of the Little Mermaid — a story with an ending that is *not* happy. So Abby and Jonah mess it up on purpose! Can they convince the mermaid to keep her tail before it's too late?

Whatever After #4: DREAM ON

Abby and Jonah are lost in Sleeping Beauty's story, along with Abby's friend Robin. Before they know it, Sleeping Beauty is wide awake and Robin is fast asleep. How will Abby and Jonah make things right?

Whatever After #5: BAD HAIR DAY

When Abby and Jonah fall into Rapunzel's story, they mess everything up by giving Rapunzel a haircut! Can they untangle this fairy tale disaster in time?

Whatever After #6: COLD as ICE

When their dog, Prince, runs through the mirror, Abby and Jonah have no choice but to follow him into the story of the Snow Queen. It's a winter wonderland . . . but the Snow Queen is mean, and she FREEZES Prince! Can Abby and Jonah save their dog . . . and themselves?

Whatever After #7: BEAUTY QUEEN

Abby and Jonah fall into the story of *Beauty and the Beast*. When Jonah is the one taken prisoner instead of Beauty, Abby has to find a way to fix this fairy tale . . . before things get pretty ugly!

Whatever After #8: ONCE upon a FROG

When Abby and Jonah fall into the story of *The Frog Prince*, they realize the princess is so rude they don't even *want* her help! But will they be able to figure out how to turn the frog back into a prince all by themselves?

Whatever After #9: GENIE in a BOTTLE

The mirror has dropped Abby and Jonah into the story of *Aladdin*! But when things go wrong with the genie, the siblings have to escape an enchanted cave, learn to fly a magic carpet, and figure out WHAT to wish for . . . so they can help Aladdin and get back home!

Whatever After #10: SUGAR and SPICE

When Abby and Johah fall into *Hansel and Gretel*, they can't wait to see the witch's cake house (yum). But they didn't count on the witch trapping them there! Can they escape and make it back to home sweet home?

Whatever After #11: TWO PEAS in a POD

When Abby lands in *The Princess and the Pea* — and has trouble falling asleep on a giant stack of mattresses — everyone in the kingdom thinks SHE is the princess they've all been waiting for. Though Abby loves the royal treatment, she and Jonah need to find a real princess to rule the kingdom . . . and get back home in time!

Whatever After #12: SEEING RED

My, what big trouble we're in! When Abby and Jonah fall into *Little Red Riding Hood*, they're determined to save Little Red and her grandma from being eaten by the big, bad wolf. But there's quite a surprise in store when the siblings arrive at Little Red's grandma's house.